Losing

MY

BREATH

J ROSE BLACK

Copyright Page

Copyright © 2023 by J Rose Black

Losing My Breath

All rights reserved. No part of this publication may be reproduced, distributed, or transmitted in any form or by any means, including photocopying, recording, or other electronic or mechanical methods, without the prior written permission of the publisher, except in the case of brief quotations embodied in critical reviews and certain other noncommercial uses permitted by copyright law.

Adherence to all applicable laws and regulations, including international, federal, state, and local governing professional licensing, business practices, advertising, and all other aspects of doing business in the US, Canada, or any other jurisdiction, is the sole responsibility of the reader and consumer.

Neither the author nor the publisher assumes any responsibility or liability whatsoever on behalf of the consumer or reader of this material. Any perceived slight of any individual or organization is purely unintentional.

ISBN: 979-8-9881823-3-7

Cover design by Mallory Rock of Rock Solid Book Design (www.RockSolid-BookDesign.com).

Free ebook

GET A COPY OF OFF THE RECORD, FREE

"It's all right, Leo. I'm just a reporter sent to interview the future Rookie of the Year. I didn't realize he'd..." She paused to pointedly stare at Breslin's towel. "...uncover so much more."

Scan the QR Code below to download Off the Record for free (hosted at BookFunnel):

Contents

"One of the most important things you can do on this earth is to let people know they are not alone."

— SHANNON L. ALDER

CHAPTER 1
First

SHE BEGAN WITH A DAY OF RAIN.

R ain drenched her hair and stuck her pale-pink blouse to her skin—in all the right places. Translucent fabric clung to her ample chest. She looked fresh-faced, and—Callan grinned—*a little cold*. She stepped into the apartment building, carrying a pocketbook in one hand and a backpack slung over one shoulder.

He leaned against the iron railing on the second floor overlooking the lobby of the sprawling downtown Chicago apartment complex. Its bare, "urban chic" decor designed to attract young professionals, the place advertised itself as being "Uptown in the midst of Downtown." But it was cheaply constructed and on the edge of the "good area" of town. He lived there because, being a former Marine, he didn't fear the criminal element. He got a decent-sized apartment for the price, and an easy commute to sporting events, the airport, and public transportation.

The population shifted every six months as life situations or jobs changed. This young woman appeared to be new. Sopping wet, she left a trail of water on the etched concrete leading to the bank of elevators. *What a mess. Someone has to clean that up.*

She stepped out into the second-floor hallway. His apartment sat along the last row of residences; a single apartment was situated across from his. They were the only two located to the right of the elevator on the northeast side of the building. He watched her glance one way and then the other before starting toward his end of the floor.

A strange flutter flapped wings in his abdomen, like the sensation of falling. *She can't be . . . Do not be my new neighbor.*

She stepped past him without a look. Proud shoulders and an upturned nose paraded past him, despite her disheveled appearance. *Really? In a place like this?* She stopped at the door just across from his apartment. *Dammit. Leasing didn't say anything.* She paused outside her door, adjusted the strap over her shoulder, and shivered.

Not this one. She doesn't even have the sense to use an umbrella in a fuckin' rainstorm.

The prissy-looking young woman pulled a set of keys from her pocketbook, and promptly dropped them on the floor. She leaned down, but the backpack slid from her shoulder. It hit the tile with a loud thud.

He grumbled under his breath, stepped forward, and swiped them from the floor. The woman righted herself, pack in place. She turned and looked at him—bright, aqua-blue eyes met his gaze and then quickly glanced away. "Thank you," she said in a soft voice. Her fingers didn't so much as graze his when she plucked the keychain from his grasp.

Yeah, that's right. Keep your distance. He nodded and turned to open his own door. Just before he shut it, he heard her call out, "Oh, you're my neighbor?"

He pivoted to look back at her. The lace of her bra peeked through the soaked material of her shirt. *It's a nice view.* Water dripped from her hair down her cheeks and looked like tears. "No. You're *my* neighbor."

"Oh, 'cause you—" Her lips pursed together and one hand went to her hip. "Ha ha." She wiped her hand on her shirt, as if that would make it any less wet. She extended it in his direction. "My name is Meridian Daly."

Nope. We are not going to be friends. He nodded and turned to shut his door.

"And you are?" her voice called out after him.

Manners, Brand. Respect others. "Your neighbor," he said through the wedge-shaped opening in the door. Meridian Daly's dark-blond hair stuck to her forehead. Her mascara trailed a black line down one side of her face. It didn't diminish her attractiveness.

Her hand returned to her side. Her brow furrowed; she tilted her head. *That's right. You don't know me. I could still be a threat.* But instead of backing away, she stepped forward, like she meant to close the gap. That strange flutter took flight in his stomach again. *Fuck.*

"Buy an umbrella." He shut the door.

CALLAN STOOD FROM HIS DESK AND CROSSED THE living room that served as his home office. He leaned his head against the window. The apartment held a stillness. An uneasy quiet. *Years of never having time alone. It's still strange, hard to get used to.*

The late-afternoon sky had already turned to dusk. Grayish-purple clouds darkened above the distant city skyline. *How long before this place, this life . . . feels real?* He let out a long breath. But it was like he didn't feel it. Wasn't involved. Just forever a distant observer of the lives other people lived.

His wrist device buzzed and chirped. He blinked and glanced at the message.

Leasing: Can you come down right now?

He sighed, scribbled something the watch interpreted as "Yes," and turned away from the window. He was used to receiving requests from the leasing office. The mostly female staff had a habit of asking for his help whenever there was someone questionable hanging around.

He flicked his wrist. *It's about time for the office to close.* He grabbed his keys from the counter and headed downstairs.

I wonder what the emergency is this time.

He let himself into the leasing office. It was the kind of place that added faux distressed brick to the walls as decoration. He hated the place, the fakeness of it most of all.

"Hey, Callan," the leasing lady greeted him from her desk. She always wore a wide smile, too perfect to be real. A dark-haired woman sat in an overstuffed chair along the opposite wall—the only other person in the place.

"You know Alice, right?" the leasing lady waved the woman over; her bracelet jingled when she shook her hand.

No, I don't know her. He remained silent. If the Marine Corps had taught him nothing else, it was: don't speak when you don't have something to say.

The dark-haired woman rose gingerly from her seat. She winced and waddled toward him, her posture stiff and strange. She hugged a plastic bag to her chest with one arm. "Hi. I hope, ah. I just wanted to return this." She shoved the sack at him. He glanced down, then back at her. *What's this?*

"I—I had it cleaned. I figured it was the least, you know, since you, ah." She ducked her head. "Took care of her. My daughter." A sniffle, and then watery dark eyes lifted to meet his gaze. "When I couldn't."

Daughter? He opened the bag. Inside was his jacket—the blue-gray windbreaker he'd left with a little girl, to protect her from the rain. He'd pulled her from a mangled car while first responders rescued the driver. *This woman's the driver.*

He nodded at the woman. "Thanks."

"It's no trouble," she said with a tight smile. "I come by here on my way to Lara's daycare. That's my daughter."

He remembered that day. Didn't he? The little girl; her image flashed in his mind. In her car seat, dressed in pink. She had wailed and screamed. Light bruising on her left temple had been a concern at the time.

But the child. A girl. The smell of gunpowder and almonds filled his nose.

"Mission, there's a child." His own voice echoed, reverberated through his skull.

A dull thump. Small gasps. Someone murmured, "Are you—are you OK?"

Callan stared at the bag on the floor. He stuffed his hands in his jeans pockets to keep them from grabbing fistfuls of hair. His breathing rushed, labored, like he'd just returned from his morning run. Red pulsed around the edges of the room.

Get a grip, Brand. It's not real. He gritted his teeth. Pain crushed his chest with blunt teeth. It took everything he had not to cry out. *Breathe.* He took a deep breath. Held it. Counted on the exhale. Another breath. A slow, controlled release. His heartbeat slowed.

He retrieved the plastic sack with his windbreaker. "I'm fine." He righted himself. Stared at the fake brick that reminded him of an old hospital building. A gray haze floated in. The world began to blur.

Alice pointed to the bag in his hand. "There's something else." She reached for the sack, then stopped. "Um? Could I? It's just, well, Lara made something for you. It's one of those crafts that you do with toddlers, but . . . I thought it might be nice."

He handed her the bag. She smoothed the plastic and unearthed a partially crumpled red piece of construction paper. A child's handprint in white paint, some glued-on blue stars. "One of the EMTs said you served."

"Yeah."

"So did my father. I thought you might like it. Like to have, you know, a keepsake. I thought the flag might—"

"Unnecessary."

Her eyes widened. She took a step back.

Shit. My tone. Dammit, try again, Brand. "It's kind of you. But you should—"

Bzzt. Her phone vibrated. She grabbed for it, gasped, shoved the thing back in her purse. "Sorry, I have to go." She pushed the bag into his arms. "I just—I don't know what I would have done if something happened to Lara. So thank you. For keeping her safe." Alice placed a hand on her back and shuffled her way to the door.

The page shook in his hand. *I can't keep this.* His stomach turned as the faint scent of smoke lingered in the air.

"Making friends?" the leasing lady's voice called out from behind him.

Callan blinked and shook his head. He tucked the child's artwork into the bag with his jacket. "I try not to," he said, and moved toward the hallway. *I need to get out of here.* He sucked in another breath, holding it as he went.

The busy, colorful community bulletin board caught his eye. Flyers wavered against their thumbtacks. Along the very edge of the board, a blurred image overtook his attention. He paused. *What the hell am I looking at? This side is a dark blob. Is that a brick pattern? Why is someone . . . That's an arm. With a tattoo. Probably. Grainy piece-of-shit photo. What's the point?*

"Oh, hey, that picture, right? A couple of residents said they've seen this guy hanging around the retail area after dark."

"He do something?"

"Not that I know of. But one person said he saw him with a knife."

"Can't tell in this."

A loud huff. "I know. But with the photo up, residents who come through here usually ask. And we tell them to be on their guard."

How hard is it to take a photo? Callan grunted.

"Glad you agree."

"A guy with a sleeve tattoo and beard, maybe carrying a knife, isn't much to go on. If I had the original image, I could try enhancing it. Take it to the police."

"Oh wow. OK, I'll text the resident, ask him to send it."

He nodded and shoved open the door with one elbow. As he exited, the leasing lady held it.

"You know, one of these days, maybe you'll let me thank you properly for always looking out for us."

He shrugged. "No trouble."

"You don't have to do anything. But you do. Just like when that accident happened last week. And you were there—helping Alice and her daughter. It's, uh, well, I know I'm not the only one who feels safer with you around." She leaned against the doorway. She crossed her arms under her breasts, lifting them so that they strained the open collar of her sweater. "Maybe dinner? I like to cook. I—I don't often because it's just me, but . . ."

Make me dinner? He lifted his gaze. Her flushed features and coy glance said volumes with just a look.

She doesn't want this fucked-up mess. How many times have the doctors told you— He turned away. *I can handle it. But no one else should have to.*

"Really, Callan?"

He stared at the ground. *What do I say? What can I say? "If you knew half of what I've done, you'd see me for what I am: a monster."*

And because he didn't have anything to say, he didn't say anything at all.

IMPOSSIBLY LONG LEGS STRETCHED FOR WHAT LOOKED like miles in short, loose running shorts. The legs and their owner caught Callan's attention on the treadmill—running beside him.

The rhythmic sound of the machine soothed him. His steps and breathing worked together to drain the color from the world. And the rage. Adding the appealing sight of a well-formed female physique layered in a hazy sense of euphoria to his meditative state.

This is the best start to a day I've had in years. He grinned and risked a glance at the owner of the legs.

The same girl: Meridian Daly, his new neighbor, wore a dark-colored workout bra with a long, sheer shirt that showed off her slim figure as she jogged.

He huffed. *Her again. Of course.* He hadn't seen her since she'd moved in a few weeks ago.

He finished the sprint on his HIIT program, and scaled back the pace to a walk. She continued her jog, her lean arms pumping as her chest rose and fell. Her torso pivoted in time with her steps.

The prissy mess does have some athleticism. Too bad she

doesn't have any sense. They finished at about the same time. Prissy Neighbor stepped off the end of her treadmill, right into his path. She stopped short and turned to look at him. The skin at the sides of her eyes folded into tiny wrinkles as her lips curved into a smile.

A warmth washed through him. He was probably still grinning like an idiot from earlier. But he felt good. *For the first time in how long—*

She met his gaze and her smile fell. "Sorry," she mumbled. Her face pinched into a scowl as she turned away.

He stared as her hot-pink sneakers trod over the dull gray carpeting. She moved toward the mirrored wall and grabbed a set of dumbbells from one of a half dozen stacks of gym equipment.

That heated flutter flapped its wings, then poked him with something sharp. *Point taken.* She lifted one weight over her head, then lowered it to her shoulder. *I could have been nicer when we met. I guess.* He shrugged.

She wiped her hand on her shirt, as if that would make it any less wet. She extended it in his direction. "My name is Meridian Daly."

He rolled his eyes. *Probably has a thing about manners.*

He moved to the nearest stack of weights. His neighbor finished her shoulder presses and set the dumbbells back on their rack. He hefted a medium-heavy set from the bottom. Endurance day meant higher reps and lower weight. He turned to place them at the end of the nearest bench.

In time to see Prissy Neighbor sit on it. He paused. She took a sip of water, then glanced up. Her cheeks flushed; her blue-green eyes sparked and danced in the fluorescent light. A small frown creased the skin between her brows.

"You're following me." He placed the dumbbells on the mat and straightened.

His neighbor rolled her eyes as she stood. "I happen to work out every Tuesday and Thursday at this time." She flipped her long ponytail over her shoulder. "This is the first time I've seen *you* here." She pointed at him with her water bottle.

Nice of her to offer. He grabbed the beverage, uncapped it, and took a nice long drink. "Thanks," he said, and handed it back.

She glared. "Are you this big of a jerk to everyone here, or do I get some special treatment for living across the hall from you?"

"I thought you were offering it to me. It's bad manners to point," he said with a chuckle.

"You're lecturing me on manners? The guy who can't even introduce himself?" The frown on her face wasn't even close to cross. She was clearly too good-natured for her own sake, and—if *their* interactions were any indication— she was also far too naïve. *She shouldn't be in a place like this. Maybe locked in some ivory princess tower, guarded by a monster.*

Prissy Neighbor huffed as she stepped around him. She bent down, in those short running shorts with the open sides—to whip a pair of fifteen-pound dumbbells off the rack.

He sighed. *Yet another one I'll need to keep an eye on.*

11

Trouble will find her. I have zero doubts about that. The only question is: How bad will it be when it does?

He grimaced. *It's like she doesn't even live in the same world. Where dark and twisted people exist, killing and preying on the weak. Innocents.* She hefted one weight up to her shoulder, turning the grip as she went. But she slung the other dumbbell—engaging back muscles and using momentum to help propel the heavy weight.

She's mad at me. So she'll end up injuring herself. He shook his head and crossed his arms over his chest. "Your form is wrong."

She met his gaze in the mirror. Sweat dripping from her temples like the rain on that day . . .

His eyes drifted to his own reflection. A hard-assed former Marine glared back. She turned her back to him and repeated the awkward movement.

He sighed. "You should lower the weight and go slower. You're slinging the dumbbell and not getting the full benefit of the effort."

Prissy Neighbor pivoted and faced the mirror again. He could see her brain processing the information. Her first instinct, the stubborn side of her, stuck out her chin and glared, again, at his reflection. But her more reasonable side must have won out. She put the dumbbell back on the rack —with a loud clatter. Then she repeated the hammer-curl movement with the lower weight.

"You'll get better results if—"

"What now?" She planted her free hand on her hip. Her lip curled into a snarl.

What do you know? She has some fight in her after all. "I can show you," he offered.

She flipped the weight to her free hand, then met his gaze. One light-colored eyebrow rose. Another wave of heat flared in his abdomen.

He moved behind her, sliding his fingers along her tricep toward her forearm. He lifted the weight from her hand and set it beside her, then held her wrist in a straight line out from her shoulder. "Hold, right there."

Warmth radiated from her skin in waves. Her pulse beneath his fingertips. The telltale flutter in her neck. Life. It mattered, was precious. And could be taken away in an instant. The urge to remain there, connected to another human being, stirred an ache in his chest. *Her hair smells like strawberries and coconuts.*

He fitted one palm against the back of her hand; the other held on to her elbow. "This isolates the bicep." He helped her complete the movement without a weight.

"One one thousand, two one thousand, three one thousand." Her knuckles tapped her shoulder. "Now down in one fluid movement."

He helped her repeat it once more before retrieving the weight at her feet. She performed eight full reps, then switched hands. She met his gaze in the mirror as she executed the same movement—working the other bicep. He gave her a slight nod, and his reflection added an even smaller smile.

After finishing sixteen reps, she lifted one side of her mouth. "Thanks, Umbrella Guy."

Umbrella? Oh. He shrugged. "I gave you good advice."

"While technically true"—she drew out the last syllable —"most people would have started with introducing themselves."

He crossed his arms against his chest and ducked his head to look her in the eye. "I'm not most people."

"Of course not. So then the same rules of politeness, of decency, just—what? Don't apply to you?"

He shrugged. *What a royal pain in the ass.*

"You should hang a sign on your door in that case. To let the rest of us know 'approach snapping, snarling neighbor with caution.'"

"Wouldn't have deterred you."

"No?"

"You seem to like inviting trouble." He leaned closer. A sprinkle of freckles dotted the bridge of her nose; those aqua-colored irises held gold flecks in their depths.

"I don't. You're projecting."

"You don't know me. I could be a stalker. Or a killer. But you gave me your name first thing—a young woman living alone, no less."

Her eyebrows rose and she straightened.

"And now you've told me exactly where you'll be at this time on Tuesdays and Thursdays. Not just me but anyone within earshot."

Prissy Neighbor uncapped her water bottle; she paused, eyeing it as if its contents had turned into mud.

"Didn't your parents teach you to think?"

That was when she dumped the rest of her water bottle out. On him.

Icy liquid splashed his face like a cold slap of her hand.

Shit! His shoulders hardened. A shudder ran the length of his spine. Water dripped and slipped down his neck. It soaked the front of his shirt.

Prissy Fuckin' Neighbor strode toward the exit. As she reached the door, she halted, turned her head.

"Buy an umbrella." She tossed the words over her shoulder, opened the door, and walked away.

CHAPTER 2

Determined"

THAT WAS A WORD FOR HER.

Callan could never explain what pulled him from sleep. In the military, rest periods were abrupt. Shoved between actions, rarely considered. But civilian life . . .

His heart raced when he came to. The room around him changed from darkness to images in an instant. He ran a hand over his face and pushed himself from the bed. Sweat stuck his T-shirt to his skin in patches. He grumbled and pulled it over his head.

Dressed and ready to run by 0500. Black coffee was the only energy drink he needed.

Callan set his route on his fitness app, clipped his key to his shorts. He glanced at Prissy Neighbor's door on his way out.

"Buy an umbrella."

She'd tossed his own words over her shoulder like it was some kind of triumph. The water had been cold, but not worth bothering over. *Just unexpected.* He moved toward the stairwell, throwing his shoulder into the door. *Can't let your guard down, Brand. You know better.*

PT completed, Callan settled down to work at 0700. He knew better than to start with his email. The thing was a mixed bag of time-suck first thing in the morning, so he usually began his day reviewing the virtual project board instead. It contained a list of tasks and subtasks and kept notes and statuses in one place.

A voicemail message from Private Number at the top of his inbox caught his attention. With a heavy breath, he pressed the "play" button, expecting to hear an automated message about a car warranty or even one of those tax schemes.

"Hey asshole, pick up the phone. It gets old talking to your voicemail. I'm trying to check in on a brother." The familiar voice of his longtime comrade Greyson Watts blared from the computer speakers. "I demand proof of life. Let's go grab a beer. Stop being a dick and call me back. You probably haven't been out since the last—"

He hit the "stop" button in an attempt to end the stabbing pain behind his eyes. *Can't stand that guy.*

Since they'd been discharged, the gregarious idiot had taken it upon himself to regularly pester Callan about unimportant shit: unofficial reunions, VA appointments, recruiting events . . .

Unlike you, I don't *miss it.* He clicked "delete" and settled into his work for the day.

Shortly after noon, his cell vibrated and lit the face of his watch.

Leasing: Hey, got the photo you asked about. Incoming.

He eyed the only slightly less terrible image on his phone. He rubbed a hand against his forehead. *I'll need help with this.*

He pulled up his chat program and sent an encrypted message to his small team of analysts. *Find the man with the knife. <attached image>*

The ensuing one-upmanship and meme fodder amused him. He received the enhanced photo of a grizzled older man. A little too lean, his eyes much too hollow. Weathered skin, a gnarly matted beard. The man's tattoo ran from his wrist to his shoulder, but the markings were much too blurred. He messaged the analyst: *No knife?*

After a few seconds, they responded: *Couldn't find one. Sorry, boss.*

I can't say the person who took the photo is the most reliable witness. He sighed and leaned back in his chair. Sent the altered image back to the leasing lady.

The leasing lady responded almost immediately. *He does look sus. I'll replace the blurry one. Thanks!*

Callan frowned at his device and messaged back. *No knife. Where was this?*

A quick, one-word response popped up: *alley*

He rolled his eyes and grumbled to himself. *Yeah, no shit.* He set his phone down on top of his desk. It vibrated again. A new message notification displayed on screen.

behind retail center

Without a visible weapon, there was no police report to be made. But at least the other residents would have a warning that this guy was lurking about within a few city blocks of their home—possibly armed. Hopefully, most people would have the sense to be on their guard anyway whenever they were out in this area. After dark.

He cast a glance at the door. *I should have told her to buy pepper spray. To go with her umbrella.*

Saturday flew by, like it always did. Callan stepped outside the main building of the Newport Heights apartment complex. His right running shoe flexed more than it should have. He glanced down and grumbled at the trailing laces. *Dammit.* He knelt and tied his shoe.

The click-clack of high heels. A high-pitched giggle. Long, sculpted feminine legs came to a halt beside him. *They look even better in heels.* He blew out a breath and rose to his feet.

"Oh. And it's you. Maybe just 'U' for Umbrella Guy with no name."

"You're not resourceful. Or you're not trying."

"I'm not trying because I really don't care. If you want to be a normal human, you'll introduce yourself. If not, the mystery shall remain unsolved. I'm fine either way."

He swallowed the urge to grin. "Maybe I can't tell you who I am."

"Ha ha. Yeah, OK. One of those 'I can't tell you or I'd

have to kill you' things." Her eyes narrowed under so much makeup. "So mysterious. So cool. Whatever." She tossed her hair and looked away. He took the opportunity to appreciate the view. Ms. Priss the neighbor wore a low-cut minidress that hugged every tight, sensual curve of her body —and showed off those legs to full advantage.

He had to admit, he was starting to enjoy this. She was emotional, expressive. *A little too easy to rile up.* But that was what made these small interactions fun.

He stuffed his hands in his pockets and glanced around. *Minidress, high heels.* "Date tonight?"

"Meeting friends." She looked at him, arms crossed, shoulders turned away. Prissy Neighbor peeked over her shoulder. "You?"

He grinned. "Can't tell you that either."

"You're such an ass. Go away already and let me wait for my rideshare in peace."

He shrugged but stayed put. A minute or two crawled past. Cool April air swept through the silence. The sound of traffic in the distance.

"I'd ask if you were waiting for a ride, too, but I figure you won't tell me."

"I'll walk."

"Over a mile?"

"You don't know where I'm going."

"I'm assuming the retail center with all the restaurants. But your secret spy base of operations could be closer than that, *I guess*," she said with a scowl and a huff.

He couldn't help it: he chuckled. A light bubbling danced in his chest. It brought a warmth, and the memory of her skin beneath his fingertips, the sweet smell of her hair. A strange urge to pull her close, to touch her hand, again, settled into the warmness of the moment.

Tires screeched as a white SUV turned off the main drive. The engine revved, accelerating through the parking lot. He moved to the edge of the curb—between the oncoming vehicle and his neighbor.

It lurched to a halt; the window rolled down. "Meridian?" The driver glanced from Callan to the overdressed woman behind him.

"Ah, yes. That's me." She held up her phone and moved toward the SUV. Callan pulled open the door; his neighbor paused midstep. She frowned up at him as she settled into her seat. "Did you need a lift?"

"Nope."

"But we're going to the same place."

"I'm fine. Have fun but stay alert." He closed the door before she could say another word.

Her eyes met his through the glass—for just an instant. She blinked long lashes, lowered her gaze, and turned away.

CALLAN STARED AT THE BARTENDER'S BACK, SILENTLY willing the man to bring him his dinner. The large screens displaying early season hockey were losing their appeal. His stomach growled like a caged and starving beast. *Come on. I thought getting here early I'd get better service. Not have to wait longer.*

"Hey, uh, sir?" a woman's voice called out from the

other end of the counter. He glanced that way, taking a quick mental snapshot of the blond hair, black minidress . . . *And it's her.* He blew out a breath. *She dressed like that for a sports bar? Gimme a break.*

He couldn't help it. He swept his eyes over the dining area behind her and found the likely group of Prissy Neighbor's friends—two tables pushed together, coed crowd teeming about the centerpiece.

The bartender turned toward her. *You should be checking on my food.* But the guy continued to ignore the mental prodding and decided the newcomer needed all of his attention. *Of course. If she asked him, he'd probably give her my food.* The lousy excuse for a server leaned over the bar and settled his chin on one hand and grinned.

Get her drink. Get my food. Leave her alone. A waiter moved into Callan's peripheral vision. The savory smell of french fries permeated the air and poked him in the stomach. The hero of the evening set a heaping plate of food on the bar with the obligatory "Here you go. Can I get you anything else?"

Finally. He flipped the bun on the double cheeseburger and ripped into the thing with his teeth. His stomach grumbled its appreciation. *So much better than the cold takeout version.* He chewed another bite. *Now, what's the score in the hockey game?*

The bar faded and blurred. Movement on the overhead screens. Skates, the puck moving at light speed. Uniform colors swirled.

"Hey. Your admirer sent you this." Lousy Bartender's irritating face came into focus. Callan blinked and found another bottle of the custom-brewed IPA this particular sports bar bragged about. *It's not worth the hype.*

"She's not hard on the eyes, you know."

"She's my neighbor."

"That hot brunette lives next door to you? Dude, I need to move in." He lifted his eyebrows as he rinsed glasses in the sink.

"She's blond. What brunette?"

"The one buying is a smokin' hot brunette, dude." The server wiped his hands on his apron. "Wait, which one's your neighbor?"

Callan sipped his newly arrived beer. "Blond. Minidress."

"Legs a mile long?"

"That's the one."

"Oh, I like looking. But something about her just hits different. Like she's—"

"High maintenance?"

Lousy Bartender stuffed his hands in his apron pockets and shrugged. He tilted his head. Callan pivoted, in time for a bold brunette to settle on the barstool next to him. Behind her, Prissy Neighbor crossed her arms. Her mouth tight, she wouldn't meet his gaze. *I don't have patience for this shit.*

"You looked like you were thirsty," Bold Brunette said, and turned her stool to face him.

Callan lifted his bottle. "Thanks. I can buy my own."

She straightened. "That wasn't what you were drinking?" She smoothed her palm over his shoulder. Her floral perfume came on as strong as she did. He fought the instinct to remove her hand in such a way that she wouldn't make the mistake again.

You can't physically harm her, Brand. "What are you doing, Daly?"

"Trying to talk her out of consulting the world's worst personal adviser and life coach," Prissy Neighbor shot back.

"Good."

"She said you're a trainer?" Bold Brunette leaned closer. Her hand slid to grasp his tricep, as if testing its density. "I really want to tone my body in time for summer. Can you help me?"

Callan inwardly groaned. *This is too much.* "I didn't give you permission." He pulled her fingers from his arm as gently as he could manage.

"What? Are you serious?"

"I told you he's super grumpy and a royal pain in the ass." Prissy Neighbor finally met his gaze. One eyebrow lifted in a smug expression.

"I'll take that as a compliment." He finished his beer and shoved it across the surface of the bar. *I need to kiss that look off her face. Brat.*

Her eyes narrowed. "It's not one."

"I thought you just meant like as your personal trainer. Aren't they supposed to be grumpy, hot, and kinda, ya know, not that bright?"

What the hell? Lousy Bartender pressed his palms together and stared at the ceiling. *Yeah, your dream, my nightmare. I need to get out of here.*

Prissy Neighbor flushed a bright red. "It's not like that. I never said he wasn't—"

"Close my tab. I'll pay for the beer." Callan handed his credit card to Lousy Bartender.

"What the fuck, Mer? What's this guy's problem?" Bold Brunette stepped down from her barstool.

"My problem?"

"I tried to explain he's not approachable." His neighbor held up her hands. "It's not my fault you didn't—"

"Not approachable? He's a downright troll. Hot on the outside, a miserable, small, and pathetic excuse of a human being inside." Bitchy Brunette spun on her heel and stalked off.

Prissy Neighbor stared at the floor. "Uh, s-sorry. She's kinda upset. She caught her boyfriend cheating last weekend and—"

"Which gives her a free pass to treat random strangers like shit." He signed his credit-card slip and crushed his copy into his pocket. "Or maybe it's OK because I'm your *personal trainer*."

"I didn't mean . . ." She knitted her hands together. "I wasn't trying to be demeaning. I just don't—I don't even know what to call you."

"So don't." He ducked his head and shouldered his way out of the bar. *Childish plastic dolls. That's all they are.* He snarled. *They have no idea what the real world is like.*

CALLAN'S BLOOD PUMPED LOUD AND HOT THROUGH HIS system. He breathed in the chilled night air, but it didn't alleviate his temper. *Fucking brat. What the hell was that?*

I'm just supposed to sleep with her friend? He grumbled under his breath. *Of course I must work for the pampered priss.* His heart thundered, drowning out the sounds of the city as he walked.

Bzzt. Bzzt. His phone vibrated in his jacket pocket. He pulled the device out and glanced at the caller ID. *Great. As if I need his sorry ass on my phone right now.* He hit the ignore button and sent Watts straight to voicemail. *He'll just keep calling,* the voice in his head reminded him. *I'm just as stubborn. I'll win in the end.*

Is it winning? Who else even bothers? He continued the slog to his apartment. *Not approachable? That's by design, sweetheart. Maybe you'll take the hint one day.*

The rhythmic beat of his bootheels against concrete pulled at his focus. He took a deep breath; thud thud thud. Let it out. Hazy air pulled the heated sting from his veins.

And when you're completely alone, will that mean you've won? Or lost?

CALLAN ARRIVED HOME. THE SIGHT OF PRISSY Neighbor's apartment set him off all over again. Heat flared through his system, pounding. Raging. *I want to punch something.* He changed shirts and headed down to the detached garage he rented. It contained his motorcycle, a tinker road bike, his various tool sets, and a punching bag—suspended in the far corner.

He strapped his gloves over his fists, growled at his inanimate opponent. *You don't listen.* He set to work, throwing an initial jab at the bag. It trembled. He hit it again.

You don't care. Punch, jab-jab. *You were wrong. Wrong!* He threw the strength of his body into another blow. *I told you not to make me take that shot.*

He continued to punch and wrestle and kick. Until he fatigued enough to struggle for air. He slumped against the concrete wall. His left hand shook. *It's in your head. There's nothing wrong. The doctors can't find anything physically wrong with you.* He tucked the appendage beneath his opposite arm, doubling over as he tried to regain his control.

Breathe, damn you. He took a shuddering breath; heat pricked at his eyes. *You can beat this. It's all just a bunch of fucked-up garbage in your head.*

"Take the shot."

"Mission, there's a child."

No! Don't listen. Don't remember. Just . . . breathe. He inhaled the cool, stagnant air; the tang of his sweat reached his nose. A choked sob racked his chest; it razed the back of his throat.

Improvise, adapt, and overcome. I will consider my surroundings, and seek to understand what's changed from my original plan. Callan forced the mantra to the front of his mind. *Whatever the circumstances, I will adapt and set a course to thrive in the face of adversity.* He took another breath. The contents of his garage hazed into vague shapes. He fell to his knees and exhaled; a light buzzing sensation hovered around his head. A gray emptiness swirled inside, wiping it all away—everything except his direct line of sight:

smooth concrete, a series of hairline cracks converging on a single depression in the floor.

I'll keep my focus on where I'm going. Not what might have been.

RAGGED AND RAW, CALLAN MADE HIS WAY BACK TO HIS apartment. *It's after midnight.* He sighed and glanced up at the second floor from the lobby. Prissy Neighbor should already be home—tucked safely, naïvely in her bed.

He paused at his door. A tingle, a nagging feeling at the base of his neck. He scrubbed a towel against his hairline. *Something feels . . . off.* He closed his eyes and listened. Nothing.

You're being paranoid. Callan plugged his key in the deadbolt. *It's a thin line between paranoia and vigilance.* He sighed and moved to the open railing overlooking the first floor. A quick scan of the surroundings. *Surprisingly quiet for a Saturday night.* He grumbled. *You're not the security guard. They can handle—*

The front door swung open. He glanced down over the edge. There she was, his pain-in-the-neck neighbor, tripping over the threshold into the front lobby. His stomach turned to lead and sank lower in his abdomen. *She's just now getting home?*

She walked with hunched shoulders. Stumbled in her heels, caught herself, and took a few rapid stutter-steps. *And she's fucking drunk.* He shook his head. *I told her—nope. She's an adult. And none of my concern.*

Callan turned to go back to his apartment. In the corner of his eye, the lobby door moved, opened again. He stopped cold in his tracks—pivoting, he stared down at the first floor.

A tall man with a lean build, a sleeve tattoo, and a long, scraggly beard stepped into the apartment building. His head whipped one direction, then the other; he crammed both hands in his pockets and moved through the open hall-way. *You don't belong here.*

Ahead of him, Meridian slowed; her hands reached for the wall and stabbed the button for the elevator. She leaned forward, bowing her head. Her ribcage in that tight minidress visibly expanded and contracted. *What are you doing?*

The rough-looking guy kept going toward the stairs. *Where's he going?* Concrete walls echoed with his heavy footsteps. The man—who could have been the guy from the bulletin-board photo—emerged from the stairwell. He leaned against the railing and waited.

A cold chill swept down Callan's spine. *You need to leave. Now. I'll text security.* He checked his pockets. *Left my phone in the garage. Shit.*

The elevator dinged. Meridian hummed as she walked. Head bowed, she swayed on her feet. Stumbling, giggling, completely oblivious to the heightened tension hovering in the air. Much less the mugger following her every move.

I'm done with this. Callan leapt across the hall. Catching her around the waist, he pulled her off her feet into a bear hug. He spun her around. "Honey, that's the wrong door. Again."

"What the hell?" She fought against his hold, kicking at his knee, shin, thigh. "Let go!"

He shoved her through the open door into his apartment. She turned, red faced; her blue-green eyes blazed. "You're kidnapping me!"

"Stay here."

"You can't—"

He shut the door on her protests. *Now to get rid of this asshole.* He took a breath. *Someone said they saw him with a knife. And your gun's still in your desk, Brand.*

The thug reached the end of the shared apartment block and froze in his tracks. He glared at Callan.

Every muscle in Callan's shoulders tensed. "Get lost."

Asshole shrugged and looked away. "Just new to the place. Still finding my way around."

"You don't live here. So get the fuck out. Don't make this mistake again."

"Mistake? Nah, I—"

"Your mistake was walking into this building."

Black, deep-set eyes darted one direction and then back. One hand drifted toward his back hip. "What're you gonna do about it?"

"Could call the cops." Callan widened his stance. Adrenaline had already kicked in; it surged through his system, spiking his senses to high alert. "Or maybe I'll finish out my workout by punching a bag of shit."

The man growled. His eyes flashed. The hand at his hip whipped around, brandishing a twelve-inch fixed-blade hunting knife.

You have no idea whom you're dealing with. "You don't want to do this."

The thug grunted and swiped at Callan. He dodged. "Your picture's on the bulletin board. You're on security footage entering the building."

Another slash and miss. "Last chance to leave with all your body parts intact."

"Fuck you." He jabbed the weapon toward Callan's neck. Callan whipped his forearm up to block the threat. He struck out with his opposite elbow, landing a quick, sharp blow to the thug's exposed throat.

The other man dropped his weapon and grabbed at his injured neck. He staggered backward, heaved audibly for air—then stumbled away.

CALLAN OPENED THE DOOR TO HIS APARTMENT. QUICK reflexes. He brought both arms up to fend off his latest assailant: Meridian Daly, aka his drunk but prissy neighbor.

Her lethal weapon: two strappy high-heeled shoes. *Seriously?* He deflected another blow. *Ow. Is she trying to use them like nunchucks? Jesus.*

"What the hell is your problem? Why can't you just leave me alone?"

"You want me to leave you alone with an armed miscreant? I could go call him back here."

"What are you—wait. Huh?"

"I told you to be careful. To stay alert. This place isn't

princess-fairytale land. You need to think, be on your guard."

"Wh-what miscreant?"

"Did you completely miss that you'd been followed home?"

She stared at him, still a bit unsteady on her feet, her eyes glazed over. He ran a hand over his face. *This one. I don't know how much of her I can take.* "Just—"

"There was s-someone following me?"

"Yeah. Recognized his photo. He'd been seen with a knife." Callan placed the thing on his counter. "I assume it was this one."

She stood with her back against his kitchen counter, arms crossed, face pale; the heavy makeup around the eyes gave her an older, smoky look.

"Is he—" She trembled as she grabbed his arm. "Is he gone? Did he see—?" Prissy Neighbor Meridian must have lost her balance, or something else. She collapsed against him—her head on his shoulder, her body pinning one arm against his side. He touched the back of her head in an awkward attempt to hold her.

Her breath on his collarbone. The warm softness of her chest. The scent of raspberries in her hair.

She should definitely sleep in my bed. But not when she's drunk. And scared. Callan sighed. "Take my room. I'll stay on the couch." He brushed a tear from her cheek. "You're safe here."

She smiled, and she was beautiful. "Thank you."

THE NEXT MORNING, HE AWOKE TO THE SOUND OF running water. Dishes clinked and clacked. Something clattered. Hard. Cabinet doors unsticking, opening, closing. Shuffling. The smell of coffee.

He lifted his head from the couch pillow and spied his prissy neighbor in his kitchen. *Is she washing dishes? Do I have dishes?*

"What are you doing?" Sleep garbled the sound of his voice; he cleared his throat.

Her head peeked around the cabinet; the overdone makeup gone, she looked her usual self. A certain part of his body noted that it liked hearing her voice, and seeing her face—even early on a Sunday morning. He glanced down at his lap; the long pole in his boxer shorts tented the blanket over his hips. *Today you decide to wake up.*

"Saying thank you."

"You said it already. You don't need to do"—he waved a hand in her direction—"that."

"You saved my life. Seems like I could do something a little nice for you." She disappeared into the kitchen again.

He stretched and stared up at the ceiling. An image of her, in that minidress from last night . . . Looking mussed after he wrestled her into his apartment. Lips quivering and begging to be kissed.

He shook his head. *We're not doing that. Not with her* . . . "I'm pretty sure you hate me."

"Hate's kinda—well, it's a *strong* word."

"Hm. Think 'unapproachable' is the nicest thing you've said. Hitting me with your shoe-nunchucks was the worst. So far."

34

"Shoe-nunchucks?" Her head ducked around the cabinet again and met his gaze. "I'll take your word on that. I guess we haven't gotten off to the best start."

He blew out a breath.

"My friend was also really shitty to you. I'm sorry. You didn't deserve that."

"Sure. Thanks."

"So, uh, yeah. Sorry."

Callan sighed and sat up. He bunched the blanket over his lap and sent a last plea to that part of his body: *I promise I'll try. With her. Just need you to stop acting like a hormonal teenage idiot who's never seen an attractive woman before.*

It finally relented.

Callan waited for her to return her attention to the dishes. He took the opportunity to stand; he found and grabbed his jeans from the floor.

"I've been thinking about it," she called out. The faucet turned off. The sound of the dishwasher closing. "And it seems kinda silly to not get along when we live across the hall from each other."

Not really. I didn't even bother with anyone who lived there before. Before you. He hefted his jeans up over his legs and turned his back as he fastened his pants. Semi-dressed, again, in a T-shirt and jeans—he made a beeline toward the coffee.

She stood at the edge of the counter. Soft eyes and a hopeful smile turned his direction. "Do you think, maybe, we could start over?"

He sighed. "You're going to be my friend now, aren't you?"

"You could try to escape, but I'm pretty determined." She grinned up at him as he approached. "So, in the interest of trying again. I'm Meridian Daly," she said, and held out her hand.

Callan looked down at it and then back at her. He didn't want to be her friend. He wanted to have her sleep in his bed, again. Naked and soft and completely out of breath.

"If you don't tell me your name, I'm going to call you Umbrella Boy in a loud voice in public places."

"Callan Brand," he said, and took her hand. She blushed, but held his gaze.

Hmm. She's got a good poker face, but I'm not actually in the friend zone. He couldn't keep his lips from turning up into a small grin.

Which she clearly mistook for something else.

"It's nice to meet you, too, Callan."

CHAPTER 3

"Surprising"

CHALLENGING TO COMPASSIONATE BUT NEVER EASY

Whether out of sheer spite or something else, Meridian continued her Tuesday and Thursday morning workout routine.

The following Tuesday after the declared de-escalation of hostilities, Callan helped her achieve the proper form on static lunges. Proving, once again, that she was far too trusting, she let her new "friend" help her align her hip and knee . . . and then he got to admire those long, graceful legs—shined with perspiration.

"Are you a trainer?" she asked him just before he stole her water bottle again.

He took a sip and shrugged. "Now you ask me? What if I'm on the list of registered sex offenders?" He handed back the bottle. She took it with narrowed eyes.

"Then I guess I'd get to try out my new self-defense classes. Well, class. I chose krav maga. I think they said the first move is supposed to be a groin strike." She started for the door, taking those shapely legs with her.

Fair. He grimaced and went after her. "I'm not a trainer. Just spent a lot of time working out."

"Misspent youth, clearly." She held the door open, standing just outside.

"My application to princess school was rejected." Callan exited the building and fell into step alongside her. "Working out was how I coped."

Sunlight peeked out from behind striped clouds and lit the early-morning sky. Autumn weather chilled the perspiration on his skin.

"Such a shame." Meridian glanced up at him out of the corner of her eye.

"What is?"

"That you didn't go to princess school. Could have learned some manners." Her blue-green eyes sparked in the sunlight. And her mouth . . . Her lips set in some smart-looking, lopsided grin, with a small dimple.

I should definitely kiss that look off her face.

"Overrated. Inefficient. And I look terrible in a tiara." Callan grabbed her water bottle and took another drink. Because he could. A quiet breeze rustled leaves on nearby trees.

She huffed and rolled her eyes. "I guess Prince Charming school was all full up on handsome jerks."

He handed back the bottle and felt his mouth stretch into a grin. "No, I got in." He held open the door to the apartment lobby and motioned for her to go first.

"Did you? I doubt it."

They walked the short distance from the entryway to the elevators. She turned left at the wall and entered the stairwell adjacent to the elevator bank. He took a longer stride to fall into step with her.

"Expelled," he said as they started up the stairs.

"Well, no wonder you couldn't get into princess school."

"As long as *you* got in, the world will continue to turn."

"'Cause *I'm* such a princess."

"Yeah. You are." He opened the door at the top of the stairs and, again, let her go first.

They emerged a short distance from the entrances to their facing apartments. Meridian paused and stood in the center of the hall. Her complexion flushed from their morning workout. Her smart mouth curved on both sides as a thin blond eyebrow arched higher than the other. He definitely needed to watch her—over her. He took a deep breath and counted as he let it out.

She opened the door to her apartment with her back. He felt the strange urge to thank her for her company, but remained silent.

She tilted her head and met his gaze. "Well, thanks for the workout tips," Meridian said with a shrug, and closed the door.

THURSDAY, MERIDIAN MUST HAVE ARRIVED A FEW minutes before him. When he entered the gym, she yelled, "Think fast!" A water bottle flew at his face.

Shit! Callan caught it.

"Nice reflexes."

His heart raced like he'd been sprinting on the treadmill. He swallowed, took a deep breath, and counted to five. The water bottle contorted in his hand. *There's no threat. Calm down.*

"Uh, are you—"

He growled at her, "You don't *do* that to someone who's seen combat, Daly."

Callan couldn't stop it; his senses heightened to the point of hyperawareness. The television playing at a low volume behind him grated on his eardrums; the sound of a treadmill in use sharpened from a low hum to an annoying whine.

The muscles in his neck and shoulders hardened. *Dammit, not now. Breathe.*

"Combat? Oh. Y-you didn't say." She came back into focus. Her eyebrows pinched together into a frown.

Callan crossed his arms and turned away. He closed his eyes and worked through *finding his breath.* He drew in air, but couldn't hold it. His lungs contracted too quickly.

"You haven't really said anything. About who you are."

"I'm not like you."

"I know," she murmured. He opened his eyes and caught a glimpse of her reflection; Meridian's hand hovered near his shoulder for several seconds before dropping back to her side.

I don't need your pity. I'll beat this. Just go.

"Ah. Anyway. I brought you a water." She moved away, grabbing a floor mat from the pegs on the wall—instead of heading to the treadmills. With him.

She knelt down on all fours and extended her right arm

and left leg at the same time—exercises he recognized as flexibility work.

Callan closed his eyes and tried again to gain control. He started by willing his heart to slow down. He had learned to master that ability in the Marines. *Slow, deep breaths. Focus on the internal sound of your heart beating. Slow. Slow. Watch. Breathe.*

Listen for the enemy.

There's no enemy. Not anymore. He opened his eyes. Meridian switched to bicycle crunches, lying on her back, those long legs pedaling in slow, graceful turns. Her blond ponytail pooled on the mat behind her.

A part of him considered what it would be like, to just dig his fingers into her hair. And watch it slip against his hands. For hours . . .

His shoulders released. His heartbeat and breathing steadied. If only the cure for his "PTSD" could be watching her work out—he might have taken the VA doctors up on their offer for treatment. *Every soldier has issues.*

Heaving a deep breath, Callan straightened his crumpled water bottle, broke the seal, and took a sip. He threw a last glance at his *friend*, then moved to the treadmill to start his high-intensity interval training.

Friday evening, a knock on Callan's door interrupted his work. He'd received a key cyber intel report from one of his analysts in Bahrain.

He opened the door to see Meridian—armed with a

couple of brown paper grocery sacks and her winning smile. He released the door handle and stepped back. She let herself in; Callan grabbed the bags of groceries from her and followed her inside.

"You look like a steak-and-potatoes guy," she said, and moved to the sink; she flipped the water on and washed her hands.

"I'm vegan." He set down the grocery bags and leaned against the cabinets—enjoying the view. Meridian wore a pair of short jean shorts and a long-sleeved purple T-shirt. As she bent over his sink, her rear rounded above nicely toned hamstrings.

"You're a lousy liar." She tossed the words over her shoulder.

"Didn't your apartment come with a kitchen?"

"It *did*." She grabbed a paper towel to wipe her hands and turned to face him. "But I thought it would be *nicer* to have dinner together."

He ran a hand through his hair. *This woman. She's cooking dinner for me?* He checked his pulse. *No, not dead, yet. But maybe I was wrong about the "prissy princess" thing. People make mistakes. And in my defense, I've never seen an angel before.*

"Make what you want."

She grinned, and retrieved a dark amber bottle with a swing-top stopper from a paper sack. "Beer?" She held it out to him.

He narrowed his eyes. "What kind?"

"Craft specialty IPA. Very hoppy."

"Hmm. I'll try it. But I don't drink alone."

"Good thing I brought a nice lager." She set a six-pack of beer on the countertop. "I can't stand IPA, but it seemed like it would suit you."

You're starting to seem like you'd suit me.

He popped open his bottle and headed back into the den to finish reading the report. Pans sang and the burner clicked and then lit. The shtuck! sound of his refrigerator door opening. Followed by the light thunk of glass against plastic when it shut. The metallic creak of his oven door.

Callan put away the report, took another sip of his beer, and moved to the dining table to watch her.

Meridian stood in his galley-style kitchen, the fluorescent light tangling in the long gold pieces of her hair. It was the first time he'd seen it down, and dry. Her fingers curled a few strands behind one ear.

The IPA tasted cold, not quite icy like he preferred. But the combination of bitter hops with the sweet, clean malt left a pleasant taste in his mouth. She finished cutting something green—which was neither steak nor potato.

"How'd you know what kind of beer I like?"

"Well, I just picked something I'd probably hate," she said as she opened a container of cream cheese, "and figured you'd like it."

"So you hate steak and potatoes?"

"No, that was just the method for beer. Steak and potatoes was a guess based on the military revelation."

He nodded and fidgeted with the stopper attached to the bottle. "Hm."

"What branch?"

"Classified."

She held the knob on his gas stove, clicking it so it would light. "Are you being a jerk right now?"

"Only a little. Doesn't seem to deter you, though."

She made a face at him, and he could picture her, as a child princess—sticking her tongue out at a playmate in her princess castle.

"Not yet. I have a habit of persistence."

"Marines." He straightened his shoulders. "MAR-SOC." He wasn't sure whether princesses knew that meant Special Operations, so he added: "Can't say more than that."

Both her eyebrows rose. She blinked, then leaned over the sink to wash her hands, again. "And now you do—fill in the blank?" She wiped her hands on his only dish towel. "For a living?"

"Babysit my neighbor."

She turned to look at him. One hand on that hip, again. "*Now* you're being a jerk."

"Only a little." He grinned around the rim of his IPA. "Still doesn't seem to deter you."

She rolled her eyes and went back to work. The smell of bacon reached his nose about the same time as the pop! and sizzle hit his ears. His stomach growled.

"I could take my steak, potatoes, and yummy IPA and go home." She spoke to the bacon and green things as she stirred them in the pan.

"Only if you plan to let me move in."

She laughed. It sounded light and airy—like sunshine parting clouds of rain. She removed the pan from the burner and scooped the bacony-green things onto a plate.

That grin. He could picture her face: it'd be a softer smile on her lips when he laid her down on his bed and settled over her.

She placed a small plate of bacon-wrapped jalapeños in front of him. The tantalizing smell wafted closer. His stomach groaned, and his mouth watered.

"You going to have some?" He wanted to be polite, to wait for her, but his stomach poked a sharp stick into his gut and demanded food.

"Mm-hmm, but still cooking. Go ahead and eat." She moved back to the counter. "Just save me one."

"Just one?"

"I brought, hopefully, enough food."

She pulled two steaks on white Styrofoam rectangles from a grocery bag and set about unwrapping them. Callan bit into a jalapeño and chewed. The combination of spicy, crisp pepper with savory bacon—and the rich cream cheese. *Best thing I've eaten all week.*

The crack and whir of a pepper grinder caught his attention. She ground a portion of pepper over each slab of meat and rubbed it in. A dash of oil. He bit into another jalapeño.

"Not that I'm picky, but how are you making the steak and potatoes?"

"I sear the steak on each side, then bake it; the potatoes, I'm cheating. I bought deli-made au gratin potatoes and just have to heat them up."

He nodded.

"I assume you eat your steak medium rare?"

"Sure. You like yours well done?"

She shook her head. "No. Horrible. You can't do that to a steak."

"Agreed."

She placed one of the hunks of meat in the sauté pan. The heady smell of a favorite meal twisted his stomach. "If it weren't for the jalapeños, I might take mine blue."

"Ick." She grimaced. "I didn't realize you were starving." She moved the seared steaks to a baking pan and bent down to place them in the oven.

"I didn't either." He admired the way her legs looked in those shorts and platform sandals. Her quadricep muscles flexed above her knee; her calf held a light ridge behind her tibia. *Not until you showed up.*

"It shouldn't take too long." She moved the length of his kitchen—toward him. Those long, lightly tanned legs stepped close enough to invade his personal space; she helped herself to one of the jalapeños.

He caught a whiff of a syrupy floral perfume; not too heavy, but sweet and rich. He fought the urge to just wrap his arm around her waist and pull her into his lap. *You're just friends, remember? Despite the fact that she's here with food and looking good enough to eat. Damn.*

Meridian moved to the counter near the stove; she leaned against it and bit into the appetizer. A hand waved at her mouth. "Hot." She took a swig from her beer.

How un-princesslike. He smiled and relaxed into his chair. And tried to wait, patiently, for dinner to be ready. "So, what's the occasion? Am I dying?"

"Are you?"

"Aren't we all?"

"Wow, you missed your calling being a Marine." She made a wry face at him. "Could've had a truly *great* career writing ironically awful greeting cards."

"Wouldn't have come with a rifle."

She rolled her eyes.

"So you come barging in here with your raw meat, potatoes, and all your questions. But you haven't told me *your* story."

"My mother taught me never to talk to strangers. It was kind of a theme. Don't talk to strangers, don't talk unless you've been given permission by the adults. Just—don't talk." Her voice lowered. "At least, not about important things."

"Sounds like a death sentence for a princess."

"I spent a good amount of time being angry at her, and my father. Then one day, he was gone. That's when all the real words came spilling out. The ones that matter." She scowled at the floor. Red streaked her features. "By then it was too late. And I was angry all over again."

There was something interesting in her admission, like there was more to the story. Something she either couldn't or wouldn't say. Her eyes flashed and her jaw flexed. Her anger covered over the hurt of whatever their family situation was. "Sounds complicated," he said, and meant it.

"Families are. I guess. Maybe it's by some intentional design. Desperate to escape the frustrations of the one we didn't choose, we go in search of our own. Hoping for something better?"

"Not exactly my area of expertise. Rifle sighting, self-defense, personal training, I've got you covered."

A light chuckle. "Good to know." Her gaze met his and held his undivided attention. A small, almost shy smile turned up the corners of her lips. It was real and settled a warm ache deep inside his chest. He didn't know what to do or say, so he remained quiet; he broke the spell entirely when he took another swig of his IPA and glanced away.

The princess pivoted. Her eyes flitted around his apartment. "With such an impressive resume, why isn't there a girlfriend in the picture?"

Callan's heart thudded outside of its usual rhythm. "Who says I don't have a girlfriend?"

"Well, *this* is definitely a bachelor's place. With your gaming equipment left out in the middle of the living room." She waved a hand at the headset and game controller discarded atop the coffee table. "And it's Friday night." She sipped at her lesser lager. "Date night. But I found you alone in your apartment."

"And here I thought I'd never get to meet the great Sherlock Holmes."

She leaned forward over the kitchen bar; the V-cut blouse revealed the tops of her breasts. "Quite frankly, my dear Watson, if you'd had a girlfriend, you wouldn't have one now."

He swallowed the urge to grin. *She's a bold one. Confident. Challenging.* "Why's that?"

"Because if you were *my* boyfriend and you let some other woman in your apartment to cook for you . . ." She shrugged her shoulders and her mouth crooked up on one side.

Could it be this easy? "By that definition, wouldn't a

woman cooking dinner for a man in his apartment on a Friday night—seem like a girlfriend?" An electric warmth swirled inside him.

She huffed. "Maybe." Meridian met his gaze and one eyebrow rose. "If the guy in question was a little less of a jerk sometimes." She took another sip of her beer.

And the answer's no. Nothing with her will ever be easy. He mentally sighed as he held her gaze. "I'll let him know."

CHAPTER 4

"Jealousy"

IS UGLY AND SMALL. LIKE RATS.

The following Monday, during the dark hours of morning, a referral client called with a priority request. Callan and his small cybersecurity team found themselves working shifts around the clock. It took time to acquire specialty foreign intel, even with a former-Marine-turned-entrepreneur's connections.

Thursday, about midmorning, Meridian texted—asking if he could take a look at her car. He responded that he was too busy. But in between calls and emails, he started contemplating what might be wrong with her vehicle. And what could happen . . .

She could get stranded. Run off the road. The brakes could fail.

By late afternoon, he caved and called in a favor from . . . Greyson Watts.

"Auto Amigos, we're your car's new BFF. What can I do for ya?" The phone connection buzzed. A loud clang rang out. Callan winced.

"I need a favor."

"Ha." Fingers snapped; the obnoxious hum quieted.

"See, you sound like this guy I know? A real pain in my ass."

Callan rubbed a hand over his forehead.

"But I know you're not him, because he never asks for favors."

Callan rolled his eyes. "I'm asking now," he said with a sigh.

"Well, ya know I owe you one." Watts's gravelly voice pitched lower. "Just don't tell me you need a kidney or some shit. I like both of mine right where they are."

"Some friend."

"Egh, it's not a kidney, is it?"

"No, I need you to come by and check out my neighbor's car." Callan crossed one arm over his chest. His encrypted mail program dinged with a new message. He placed his phone down, set it on speaker, and turned most of his attention back to his work. "Think you can handle it?"

A loud chuckle sounded through the phone. "Gee, when ya ask for favors, you really go all out on the flattery, don't ya?"

"You don't need flattery. You're a Marine."

"Yeah, yeah, yeah. Semper fi. And in case you were wondering, I'm flipping you off right now."

"I wasn't. Back to the—"

"You doing all right, man? You've been ducking my calls *again*. Been having to keep an eye out for news stories about a body found in an apartment, due to the smell."

Callan sighed. "Fine. Just—"

"Just busy. Yeah. Same excuse. You'd save me a lot of grief if you'd go for your eval."

This is why I don't answer your calls. "I'm fine." Callan gritted his teeth. *I'm not damaged. I'm not weak.*

"You're stubborn as fuck is what you are."

Callan grunted into the phone.

"I'll swing by tomorrow."

Thanks. The word stuck to his tongue and wouldn't come out.

"But feel privileged, 'cause I don't do house calls for just anyone, you know."

"Yeah, got it." He refocused on the email. The dark-web report on his new neighbor—a personal project he'd commissioned from a US-based source—amounted to just a few paragraphs.

"Heh heh, yep. That's what I'm here for. You're wel—"

Callan terminated the connection.

- Current Employer: Zero-One Communications.
- Current Position: Public Relations Analyst.
- Marital Status: Single.
- College: Weybridge University.
- High School: Saint Anthony's Private Academy.
- Middle School: Cordray Junior High.
- Elementary: Dart Elementary.
- Parents: (adoptive) Michael Daly, deceased; (adoptive) Yvonne Daly, living.
- Adoption status: Closed.

Boring. Mostly. Boring is good. A tight band gripped his chest. *It's general reconnaissance, nothing more.* He stared at the blinking cursor on his screen. *She'll understand when I explain it. The DoD doesn't care if it's an invasion of privacy.*

He rubbed a hand over his forehead. *You've gone soft, Brand. If she's going to stick around. . . Fuck it, they could investigate her just for living across the hall.* He typed a note back to the analyst: "See what you can find out about the adoption."

He closed his laptop and pushed his chair away from his desk. *I wonder how much she knows about it.*

He texted Meridian later that evening. *A friend will stop by tomorrow and take a look at your car. After work.*

A few minutes ticked by before his phone buzzed with a response: THANK YOU! 🤍🙏

He texted back. *You're welcome, princess.*

Callan huffed a loud breath and glanced at the time. Another twelve-hour workday. Some days, it really sucked being "the boss." He closed his laptop; he needed to sleep, now, so he could be awake when Europe came back online —in a few hours.

The air in his apartment held a fresh chill. A faint burning smell caught his attention as the furnace kicked on for the first time this season.

His cell phone vibrated. Another message from Meridian popped up. *Goodnight, umbrella boy.* 🛌 🦎 😐

Callan grumbled and texted back: *That's Prince Charming to you.*

He stood and stretched. He held the phone and made his way from the den to his bedroom—before flopping on the bed. Another message popped up.

Nope! You flunked out. 💀 ❌ *No wonder you ended up a Marine.* 🥾

😉

Hmm. She should just come over so I can kiss that smirk off her face. And then do more satisfying things. He sighed and pushed the thought from his head—for at least a good minute or two.

Thanks for making me dinner the other night. Make sure your door's locked.

Callan lay down in his bed. Flannel sheets soothed against his skin—and held in heat during this time of the year. But the gray plaid appeared threadbare in places.

His phone buzzed. He read the message from his princess.

You're welcome. Couldn't let you starve. Good night. 🌙

He placed the phone down and settled into his pillow. A last thought marched with heavy legs through his brain: *I should get nicer sheets if I'm going to invite a princess to . . .*

THE FOLLOWING EVENING CALLAN FORCED HIMSELF TO put down his work and step away from his computer. He checked his watch and decided to go downstairs—to check in on Prissy Princess, her car, and his *buddy*.

Meridian had mentioned having a friend of her own stop by. He'd caught a glimpse of her in the hall: a short thing with cropped dark-brown hair and a spirited smile.

They're fine. They're adults. They don't need you to play host or run interference. Watts—for all his many, many faults—can manage this. Or I'll kill him later, which he knows, so he won't fuck it up. The former Marine was a mechanical wiz; he'd opened his own shop after being discharged by the Corps. Auto Amigos specialized in muscle-car restorations—or so Callan was told when his *buddy* showed up for a "house call"—on Meridian's ordinary Honda Civic.

I just want to check in.

He took the rear stairs and exited behind the building. Her electric-blue car sat in the mostly vacant parking lot on the back side of the apartment complex. Bright work lights stationed on either end of the vehicle lit the area almost like broad daylight.

A long, green fabric overhang jutted out from the apartment building—spanning the distance from the apartment entrance to the parking lot. At the end of the covered walk, the two women sat on the curb. Meridian leaned back against a metal post holding up the overhang, her long legs covered in jeans that ended at the top of what women considered "boots." With heels.

Meridian's friend sat a few feet away, a gas-station coffee cup balanced on her leg.

He made his way toward them, intending to do the civilized thing and make conversation. He drew up short when his princess let out a loud giggle.

"Oh my God." Meridian's friend gasped. "I don't know what he's fixing, but mine just broke."

His princess laughed. "I can't believe he's shirtless in this weather. I mean, he's been really nice. I'm thankful he could help." Meridian pulled the zipper on her jacket and stuffed her hands in her pockets. "Callan's been so busy at work the past few days."

"Forget your *neighbor*! That *can't* be a good idea," the other woman said, and pointed with her coffee cup. "And seriously. That guy." She hooked a thumb at Watts. The former Marine wore black jeans, combat boots, and nothing else. "Is a fine specimen of man." She sipped her drink and shot Meridian a wide grin.

Things I can't unhear. Or wash out of my brain . . . with bleach.

"Nora!" His princess shook her head.

"What? Look at him. Just look! At those perfectly sculpted lats. I'm digging the black tactical jeans and combat boots. And that religious-death-themed tattoo." She bit her lip and raised her eyebrows. Nora looked like a little girl pleading with her mom to let her bring home a stray puppy.

Which, when talking about Greyson Watts, was a fair comparison. If the puppy were a mongrel beast covered in fleas. *I should have fixed it myself.*

"I'm not complaining about the view. But what's with the braid?" Meridian shrugged her shoulders. "Isn't that odd for a *Marine*?"

"If you're not interested . . ." Nora trailed off. Her lips parted and formed something like an *Oh*.

Callan glanced up in time to see Watts pull his "stretch and flex move," the one he used to brag could charm any woman. *What an idiot.* He rolled his eyes, but had to admit —it did seem to have the desired effect on the two women. *And now I'm glad I haven't eaten. There's nothing to throw up.*

"What was I saying?" Nora said with a sigh. "Oh. Yeah. If you're not interested in that guy? First, you should have your head examined. And second." She grinned beneath knitted eyebrows. "I'm going to remove the spark plugs in my car and see if he'll just take me home," she said with a wink.

"Nora, you're terrible."

"Think it'll work?"

Meridian shook her head and giggled. Grown women, giggling like schoolgirls. He scowled. *Please tell me she's got better taste than Watts.*

Callan strode past the two women. He stopped a few feet away from his *buddy*. Watts bent over the front of the Civic.

A solid chill hung in the air—with the faint scent of pine. The former Marine—the one who grew his hair into a foot-long braid after he got out of the Corps, because he "hated all the haircuts"—worked at something in the front of the engine compartment. A bit of grease stained one bicep. A large black cross tattoo covered the side of Watts's ribcage; it read "Death before dishonor."

"Oh! Hey!" Watts straightened. And stretched. He threw a look over his shoulder at his audience.

Callan seethed under his breath. His *buddy* met his gaze and cringed.

"You look like you haven't had enough coffee today. And you know my rule."

"I've had my coffee for the day. And I'm still going to be scary. And you'll talk to me anyway."

"Nope. Nuh-uh." Watts crossed his arms over his chest. "I'll talk to Meridian. She's nice." He leaned forward and grinned. "And hot! Holy hell, how'd you get her as a neighbor?"

Callan glowered.

"Ohhhh-ho!" His dark eyebrows knit together. For a late-twenties former Marine, the guy still had plump cheeks, complete with a dimple when he grinned. "That's why you asked for a favor!"

"I was busy. She needed help."

"And what, you run a new handyman service for your apartment complex? Nope, not buying it." He moved his head to peer around Callan. "You want those delicious legs wrapped around you while she pants out your name."

"Stop looking at her."

"And you just proved my point." Watts shrugged. "Her friend's pretty cute, though. I think I'll flex a few more times and then ask her to go have a drink with me." An irritating smirk settled on the other man's lips.

"What's the deal with her car?" Callan shoved his hands in his pockets.

"Needs a tune-up. New timing belt, water pump. She's due." He lugged the old battery out from under the hood and placed it on the ground. "For the moment, a new battery will do the trick. Brought one from my shop, just in case."

Callan nodded.

"I'll install it, reset the radio, and she'll be good to go. But your girlfriend should still bring it by when she can—to get the other stuff done." He shrugged. "Not my usual thing, but I'll do the work. Since she's *your* girl."

"Just give me the bill."

"Same old Brand." Watts leaned back against the driver's-side door. "So, you two wanna grab a drink with me and the friend?"

"What makes you sure her friend will say yes?"

"The same thing that makes me sure you'll say no."

"Hm."

"I wish you would take me up on my offer. But at least you're not so"—Watts frowned and looked over at the two women—"alone anymore."

Callan shrugged and stared at the ground. "She suits me."

"Welp! They say there's someone for everyone." Watts picked up the used battery and started toward his black-on-black Dodge Charger. "I just figured yours was like one of those old school nuns that used to rap my knuckles with a ruler—back when I was a kid." He ducked into the front seat and emerged a few seconds later with a new car battery.

"Those rulers stung like a sonofabitch!" He hefted the battery into the Civic's engine compartment. The mechanic stretched and flexed again. "Tell me the truth, are they lookin'?" Watts gave him a wide grin.

Callan's knuckles itched to punch him. He snarled. "I think we should meet for one of our old sparring sessions."

"Yeah. No." The smile fell from Watts's features and he grazed a hand over his ribs. "I do *not* miss those. *Buddy.*"

CALLAN COULDN'T HANG AROUND. WATTS TEXTED later to let him know the friend had indeed accepted his invitation to drinks. The message ended with an emoji flipping Callan the bird.

The next message arrived with an image of a napkin; someone had written: "Being this awesome: Priceless. One 5-year car battery: $150."

Same old Watts.

Later that evening, Callan's phone buzzed again. This time, the message held a picture his friend must have taken while still at the apartment complex. The image depicted Meridian, leaning back against one of the posts in the parking lot.

Her blond hair had come down, out of the ponytail, and fell in loose waves over her shoulders.

A gentle smile on her lips, she stared at a point beyond the scope of the picture. The weak lights behind her combined with Watts's lowlight lens—captured her likeness with an ethereal glow.

An angel wearing a hoodie and jeans.

Watts typed one line beneath the picture: *Ask her out.*

Callan sighed and ran a hand through his hair. He stared up at his bedroom ceiling. *Yeah, I should do that.* He sighed. *Or maybe I shouldn't.*

He groaned. Part of him had hoped his princess would stay overnight after cooking him dinner. But the message in their playful banter was clear—Meridian wasn't going to invite herself in and take up residence in his life. She would make him work for it. For her.

"Wouldn't a woman cooking dinner for a man in his apartment on a Friday night—seem like a girlfriend?"

She huffed. "If the guy in question was a little less of a jerk sometimes."

He flopped over on his side. *Every day is a battle. Still. She doesn't need this . . . this mess. The nightmares. She doesn't deserve what I'd put her through. And she probably wouldn't stick around anyway.*

Who would?

He grumbled and pulled the pillow over his head, as if it could block out his own thoughts.

She's safer where she is . . . They worked out together twice a week, ran into each other on occasion, exchanged phone numbers "just in case." Random texts sent here and there.

Most of the time, she reached out during the long four days between Thursday's and Tuesday's workouts. *Anyone who gets too close . . .*

Fuck. You can't, asshole. And you're not being fair. Flirting with her, wanting her . . .

His heart twisted in his chest.

You know your purpose. You took an oath. Protecting people is the only thing you've ever been good at. So do it.

His cell phone lit on his nightstand; it vibrated against the surface. A message from Meridian appeared on screen. *Not sure if you're still up, but thanks. Your friend was really helpful.* 🦇

Callan sighed and typed back: *You're welcome.*

He sent the message and placed his phone down. *That's the end of it.* But before he fully settled down, his phone buzzed again.

Did you eat something? I ordered too much pizza. I know you can get caught up at work and forget to eat.

A sharp phantom knife stabbed Callan's lungs—shoving the air out of his body. He closed his eyes, drew in a breath, and counted. He replied: *I already ate.*

You're still a lousy liar. 😜

Callan shook his head. They didn't send emojis in the Corps. Such a weird addition to adult communication. Before he could respond, another message appeared.

I'll leave the pizza in a ziplock next to your door. No judgment. 🍕

He clamped his eyes shut and waited for the pang of something he could no longer name to subside; it plucked at steel threads holding him together and reverberated through his system. He should have said thank you; he should have just walked across the hall and banged on her door until she let him in—really let him in—to her life.

And then he should have kissed her.

But Marines never say die.

That's how we get rats, Meridian.

CHAPTER 5
"*Stubborn*"

BECAUSE OXEN MOVE FASTER. AND ARE MORE CHANGEABLE.

Over the next few weeks, Callan managed to surreptitiously detach from Prissy Princess. Longer lapses between texts. Shorter responses. It should have bothered him how easy it was to let go. Maybe it did. But there was a time before her. And time would pass the same after she moved on. People, like events, tended to mark the passage of time along the roadways of life.

His mother and sister, they marked the end of childhood. His father, the beginning of his adult life and independence. Odin . . . a loss of faith, probably. Something changed that day. But he couldn't settle on what that thing was. He was a person, a friend. And one minute, he was alive and angry and yelling. Then, in the blink of an eye, he just *wasn't*.

"*You're a Goddamned idiot, Brand!*" *Odin pitched his cigarette at the ground. He grasped his rifle and moved into the low ready position. A blast of dry desert air kicked up dust and sand. That tingling feeling bit at the back of Callan's neck.*

His longtime friend continued to grouse over his shoulder as he paced along the edge of the dirt path. "Why the hell are we even friends? Can I—"

BOOM! An invisible force threw Callan to the ground, knocking the wind out of him, crushing his chest, his lungs. Black smoke poured like liquid over the ground. He choked and heaved. The world pitched deadly quiet. He crawled, tried to gain his feet, only to be thrown back down again.

He shook the vision away. *Stop. He's gone. Just stop.* He shuddered and closed his eyes. Some of the memories had lost their sting over the years. Without faces . . . Faces weren't as complete or distinct, anymore. Memory was like that. Eroding bit by bit until it just turned blank.

Meridian would fade at some point, too. That was life: a ghostly march to the end. Days slipped past in the outside world. Reflections of life, of lives that other people lived.

He pushed at the gray haze that clouded his mind and focused on his laptop, again. In cyberspace, there was still an enemy to fight. He had a job to do: reconnaissance. Recommend defensive strategies. Coordinate counter-attacks.

But no more killing.

His hand shook on the keyboard. *No. Not again. This goes nowhere. Accomplishes nothing.* He closed his laptop. *I need to get out of here. Go for a walk, a ride, something. I'm getting stuck in my own fuckin' head.*

He'd take his 750cc Shadow out for a ride in the crisp autumn air. Stop by the bike shop. *Just do something normal, Brand. It's all starting to blur together again . . . like nothing's real.*

He grabbed his keys and headed for the garage.

CALLAN PULLED HIS MOTORCYCLE INTO HIS DETACHED garage, turned off the bike. The ride had helped shove the empty sense of hopelessness back into the far corner of his mind. He checked his phone for the time. *Almost midnight.* A message notification hovered on the screen.

He opened it, and read the message from her royal highness.

Missed you this week. 😔

He caught himself against the wall of the garage. *No. No no no. You're not supposed to notice. Or care.* An urge, impetus, a thriving need arose within him—to march straight up to her apartment and yell at her until common sense finally sank into her brain. *You're better off staying away from me. Why can't you see that?*

But how could he explain? If there was some disfiguring scar or something he could point to, something tangible . . .

Dammit. I function. I have purpose. I've saved lives. Served my country. That's worth something. He ran a hand over his face to wake himself up. *She's still a bad idea. She needs something, someone I can't be. Accept it and move on, Brand. She's only being nice. Because you protected her.*

Morning sunlight played on her features. A soft gleam lit her eyes. "You saved my life. Seems like I could do something a little nice for you."

69

He righted himself with a groan and headed toward his apartment. *On that topic, she's too Goddamned nice to people she has no business being nice to. How many times have I behaved like an outright jerk to her? And she responds by making me dinner. What a class act I am.*

Meridian pivoted; her eyes flitted around his apartment. "With such an impressive resume, why isn't there a girl-friend in the picture?"

Callan sighed. *Odin would've kicked my ass from here to Mexico . . . if he was still around. He'd tell me I'm a fuckin' dumbass.*

He grumbled at himself. His phone buzzed again. He stopped to unlock his phone and retrieve the message.

I guess I need to hire a new trainer? 😐

He seethed at the message through clenched teeth. *The fuck?* An image of her working out with a faceless moron, like that bartender from the other night—it taunted his brain. He almost dropped the phone. *You have no right—*

As he stepped into the stairwell, her familiar voice reached his ears. He stopped short, backpedaled a couple of steps, and peered around the corner.

Meridian strode in strappy heels toward the elevator. Some privileged-looking *dude* in his midtwenties slouched beside her. Sloucher's sandy-brown hair sat on top of his head in a man bun; he wore khaki pants and flip-flops. *It's almost November. What a douchebag.* The other man's eyes darted around, hands shoved in pants pockets. His lips twisted into a sly smile that Callan wanted to knock off his face and into next week.

His breath came in short gasps, as if he'd run from the

garage and around the block a few times before walking in the door. He sucked in a long, deep breath and held it. Red swirled across his vision. *It's none of my business*, he told himself, and tried to swallow it.

A shudder ran through his shoulders. *She* just *texted me. So who is that guy?* He started up the steps.

He arrived on the second floor, took the few steps around the corner, and stopped at his door. The elevator dinged and he heard her voice, again.

"It was really nice of you to walk me home."

"No problem. Can't have a pretty lady like you walking home by yourself."

Callan gripped the door handle and tried to erase the image of that guy's face. The way the slouchy douchebag looked at her turned his stomach. He pressed his door open.

"Um, so, yeah, thanks. I'm OK from here."

Callan halted in the doorway. *That's a brush-off.*

"I'll see you at work tomorrow. Same as usual. Right?"

Meridian gave Douchebag a quick hug, then turned away. Callan couldn't see her mouth to read her lips, but he read her body language: she wasn't interested. She was just nice. Too damned nice—all the time.

The hair at the base of his neck tingled . . . that weird feeling he'd sometimes get just before a firefight. He took a breath, let it out. Another. The world sharpened, focused.

Meridian plugged her key into the lock on her door. Douchebag hovered . . . too close.

She glanced over her shoulder, but recoiled when she saw her escort behind her. She gave him a tight-lipped smile. Her hand shook as she turned the key, unlocked the door, and shoved it open.

Alarm rose like so much acidic bile—moving the wrong way up his throat. Before Meridian could set foot into her apartment, Douchebag grabbed her shoulders!

A cry of surprise tore from her lips. "What are—"

He clamped his mouth over hers.

Callan's knuckles cracked. *She said she takes self-defense classes. I'm just here for backup.*

Meridian shoved at Douchebag's chest. She kicked him in the shins. He ducked, grabbed for her waist. She rammed her knee into her assailant's groin. He cried out, but lunged forward, knocking her off-balance.

A red haze fell over Callan's vision. The scene blurred.

"You bitch!" Douchebag hauled Meridian up to her feet by her hair. She landed an elbow to the guy's chest. Her attacker held tight.

Callan advanced. He gripped Douchebag's hand and wrist, forcibly removing it from Meridian's hair. He pulled her free, then pushed her into her apartment.

"Lock the fucking door!" He slammed it shut once she was inside. He turned.

Douchebag leaned against the wall; he groaned. "You broke my finger, asshole."

"You should run." Callan gave him one warning more than the piece of shit deserved.

"What gives, man? I'm her boyfriend. She likes to play rough—"

A satisfying crunch filled his ears. The thrill of landing a solid punch sang through his muscles. His veins.

Douchebag hollered as he sank to the floor. Callan dragged him up again, propping his new less-than-human punching bag up against the wall.

"Callan! Stop, *please!*" Meridian's voice filtered into his ear. Another voice yelled back. It was his.

"I'll break him into pieces. He's nothing but human garbage."

Meridian grabbed Callan from behind, locking her arms around his chest. He blinked and the world shifted, widened. Douchebag sagged against the wall, sniveling. Blood trickled from his nose. One eye was swollen almost completely shut.

"Please, Callan."

He snarled at her attacker. "Leave. *Now.*"

"Meridian! Let me in." Callan slammed his fist against her door.

"No. Not until you calm down."

Red flared in his peripheral vision. The world pulsed in time with his heart. "Not until I— Goddammit!" He kicked and the door jarred. Metal scraped against metal, but the thing held in place. "Open this door."

Meridian inched her door open; her eyes peeked over the safety block. She met his gaze and slammed it shut.

"No," she yelled again.

He rested his forehead against the door and gulped breaths of air. "At least tell me if you're OK."

"Am I OK? How am I supposed to know if I'm OK?" Her voice trembled. The sound provoked him all over again.

I need to see her. I need to know she's not hurt. I swear to God this'll never happen to her again. "You need to call the police. He deserves to be locked in a pen like an animal!"

"He's a coworker. He offered to walk me home. I thought he was being nice! I'm just supposed to have him arrested? And then what? How do I explain everything at work?"

"I don't care what happens to him. What people think. I'll call them myself if you don't come out, right now!"

"You're a jerk, Brand." A couple of light thuds: the sound of her smaller fists against the other side of her door. "You've always been a jerk, and you're too stubborn to change!"

He ground his teeth together. The sound of her cry still echoed in his ears. "I'm stubborn? I'm not the stubborn one. How many times have I told you?" His voice cracked as he continued to shout. His throat reminded him he'd been yelling for a while. "You're too trusting. We don't live in some fairytale where you get to flit about like a princess."

He continued to pound on the door. "We live in the middle of a city. With crime. And the human equivalent of rats."

"Is there *anyone* I can trust in your world?"

"No. You can't blindly trust anyone." Callan fell back against her door and ran a hand through his hair. He took a shaking breath. She was right: he needed to calm the fuck down.

"Not even you?"

74

A deep breath. *Hold it in. Count to ten. Let it out.* "Not even me."

More thuds. Vibrations coursed through the door at his back. A sniffle. A sob. "I can't live like that. I can't. I won't. I need to believe in people. That some are . . . good. Some strive to be better. Like you."

He hung his head. *That's not how the world works. A black, warped sickness chips away at the good things, good people. Tries to steal their light.*

Then a soft: "I believe in *you*, Callan."

Those words. He'd never heard them said like that. Like they meant something. Not the snide yell of a drill sergeant. Not the oorah before an op.

He continued his breathing; his heartbeat slowed from a blind rush to a gallop.

"But you can't just show up and be some nice-guy hero and still push me away all the time. You're confusing and I hate it!"

I can't do more than this. Don't ask me. If you ask, I'll try and I'll fail. You'll end up hating me. And I'd rather die . . . than have you hate me. Or disappoint you. My own darkness, it still chips away at me.

"It's a full-time job protecting you, Meridian." He sank to the floor, drew one knee up, and sat in the bland chaos of the moment. Breathing. "Anything more, and you'd be the death of me."

"Protecting me?" The door moved. Then she was there. Hand on one hip, her eyes puffy and red. Tears stained her cheeks.

He found his feet. His arms ached to hold her.

"I really need a—what, a bodyguard? Because I'm too *dumb* to fend for myself?" Her complexion heated from pale to mottled red. "Too helpless? Clearly, I'm a weak, naive little girl because I don't assume everyone—my coworker, for Chrissakes, Callan—is a predator?"

Light flashed in her eyes. In fact, it clung to her—flaring around her skin, her hair, her whole body. It was a trick of the eyes, his mind, when adrenaline hit his system. But she glowed. Vivid. Alive.

And for a moment, he'd have given anything to be like her.

"Just a little girl who needs her Goddamned next-door neighbor and overgrown Boy Scout to take care of her!" She trembled all over, but whether it was from anger or fear, he didn't know.

A switch flipped, kicking off an old training reel in his head. *Comfort, don't blame. Support. Be safe. Get them to report the attack.* He squared his shoulders. "No. Not dumb. Not helpless."

Icy waters swirled around him, leaching heat from his system—like he'd been treading water past his limit. He started to sink. *You'll fail. She'll hate you. Isn't it better, isn't she safer, not getting involved?*

"You're"—he tucked a piece of her hair behind her ear—"too kind. Beautiful." He tilted her head to make her look at him. A shudder ran through her; she met his gaze.

"I've seen too many terrible things."

"It hasn't changed . . . who you are." Warm, aquamarine eyes stared into him—providing a lifeline to shore. And he wondered if she was really the one who needed saving . . .

He cupped the back of her head. He moved pieces of wet hair from where they stuck to her cheek. *And it almost happened to you.* A distant pang. A sense of loss. How could she make him feel . . .

Callan leaned forward and pulled her to him at the same time. He settled his mouth over hers. Her lips curved, then pressed against his. A slow, gentle connection. Soothing. Necessary.

He moved them out of the hallway, into her apartment, and toed the door with his boot. Her palms flat against his shoulders, he wrapped his arms around her waist, pulling her closer. Fitting her against him, he brought his mouth down over hers, again.

The tears on her cheek wet his jaw. Her lips tasted warm and sweet. A trace of perfume wafted from her neck, smelling of cinnamon and citrus. He brought his hands up to cup her face as his mouth left hers to kiss her cheeks, her eyes, her forehead. Her eyes closed, more tears escaping her lashes.

Meridian's arms slid up his back; her hands clutched his shirt between his shoulder blades. He held her while she sobbed.

Lean on me when you need to. I won't let you fall.

Moments passed. The tremors coursing through her . . . lessened.

"Did he hurt you?"

"No. He just—he scared me." She shuddered. "And then you. You looked like you were going to really hurt him. And that's not like you." A watery smile stretched her lips; she wiped at her eyes. "He must have scared you, too."

"Why are you angry with me?"

"I just . . . Y-you kept yelling at me. Like I did this. Like I would ever want . . . that. And if you—who *saw* what he did—if you saw it and thought I was somehow to blame . . . what would anyone else think?"

"It's not your fault." He shook his head. "It's *not* your fault."

"I don't know what I'm going to do. At work, tomorrow."

"He'll probably call in sick. Monday's another story, but. We'll figure it out by then."

"I've never seen you like that before." She lifted her head. "Were you? Were you afraid for me, Callan?"

The room shrank; the oxygen evaporated and left only heated, unbreathable air. Her palm against his cheek. Warm eyes; an indescribable expression. Gentle, searching. Questions he couldn't answer. He did the only thing that made any sense—and kissed her, again.

Their lips met in a slow, languid kiss. Salt from her tears mixed with her natural sweetness. She wrapped her arms around his neck and pressed closer. Her softness, her scent, *she* filled and overran his senses. He mouthed another kiss against her lips. Heat flared inside his abdomen when she opened her mouth, and kissed him back with firmer lips.

He sank into her embrace, the heated connection she offered. A kinetic warmth surged through him, lighting, igniting dormant pieces inside—like someone returning home . . . A soft groan, hushed breaths. Their mouths parted and found each other again. He slid his hand behind her neck as he deepened the kiss.

Strands of hair slipped through his fingers. Meridian broke away. She pressed her forehead against his neck. Her breath warmed his skin and breathed life into his chest.

He left his arm around her, keeping her near. *Don't ask me. Don't ask me to . . . let go.*

CALLAN SAT AT HER KITCHEN TABLE AND STARED AT HIS hands. Calloused, bumpy, coarse.

Thwack. A pack of brightly colored cards landed in the center of the tablecloth. He stared. "Uno? That's the best you could do?"

"I couldn't find regular playing cards. Suck it up and deal." Meridian sat down across from him, palms flat on the table; her fingers trembled. She laced them together, tapped her thumbs. She sat still for a grand total of two seconds, and then was up again.

He sighed and reached for the pack of cards. *She's still anxious he'll come back.*

"Want something to drink?"

"Water's fine." Callan sorted out the instructions and flipped through the deck. *One round. Help her settle down. I can't stay. I shouldn't stay.*

"Do you remember how to play?"

"Sure, we played Uno all the time on base."

"Really? Odd. Doesn't seem like a hardcore Marine kinda game. But I have heard—" She met his gaze as she set the water bottle in front of him. "You're—that was sarcasm."

He swallowed a grin. "We didn't play Uno. We played

the craziest poker rules we could find. CHORSE, guts, blind man's bluff."

"Uno was too intimidating, huh?"

"Yeah. That reverse card, it's a killer." He dealt fourteen cards between them, then stacked the remainder in the center of the table.

Meridian studied her hand, moving cards into some kind of order. She flipped over the top card from the stack to begin the discard pile. He glanced at his, then laid them face down.

"Oh come on, admit it. This is the most fun you've had on a Thursday night in . . . how long?"

"Fun. Yeah." He shook his head. "Not really."

"You got in a fight. You won. And now you're playing your new favorite card game."

"My idea was better." He grinned around the mouth of his water bottle.

"Strip poker? No. I'm not the kind of girl who gets naked on a first date."

Callan almost spit out his drink. "I told you. You could keep your clothes on. If I lost, I'd strip. Hell, if I won, I'd strip. You'd win and win."

"I've never understood why men are so eager to be naked." She settled her chin on one hand. "Just randomly naked."

He shrugged. The discard pile was yellow. He grumbled and picked a card. And another. And another. He drew a yellow six and played it.

"In appropriate unmentionables, I assume male anatomy is tucked away and mostly manageable." She pulled a card from her fan and placed it in the discard pile. "Untucked and dangling just seems like, I dunno."

I know I don't say much, but I have no words right now. Dangling?

"A nuisance. Something between an impediment and a small child."

"If you're trying to distract me, it's working. I don't like to brag, but I can't claim it's as big as a child."

She blinked at him. One eyebrow lifted. "Oh, ha ha. No, I mean, it's always ready to tell on you for every dirty thought."

He rubbed a hand over his forehead. "You've been dating the wrong guys. No, strike that. You haven't been with a real man." He played a wild card and ditched a green five.

"Mm. I'd agree with that." She drew several cards before turning over something playable. "My last boyfriend? Well."

"Could only dream of being Prince Charming's lackey is my guess."

"It's a long story. Not worth the time or energy." She narrowed her eyes and drew more cards. "He was a year ahead of me in high school. I thought I was *so in love*. I was really just *so dumb*." She sighed and drew another card. "Ha! Reverse. You lose a turn."

"Devastating."

She played two cards. "Once he went away to college, he was done. He had no time for me. But I chased after him, trying to make things work."

"That was your last boyfriend?"

"I've dated since then. I was busy, though. And honestly, between Jase and my father . . . I got pretty tired of men who wouldn't make time for me or the things I feel are important." She shrugged. "So most of my college dates didn't make it to boyfriend status."

"Like I said: you haven't been dating real men." He played his second to last card. "Uno."

"Dammit." She glared at him. "You were distracting me." She pulled a card from her fan and played it. He grinned and tossed his last card in the pile.

"If we'd played my game, could've done a better job."

She rolled her eyes, but giggled. Callan rose from his chair. *Time to go.*

She followed him to the door. "Thank you for playing a silly game with me. In the middle of the night no less." Her smile wobbled; she looked away.

"It's important you feel safe. If you want me to stay, I can take the couch while you get some rest."

"You can be really sweet." She moved closer. He took the hint and tucked his arm around her waist. "In your own way."

"No. I can only be intensely loyal, protective, and, when necessary: lethal. None of it's *sweet*, but it is honest."

"I like honest. Honest is good." She smiled up at him with bleary eyes.

He released her and opened the door.

"You going to keep hiding from me?"

Callan sighed. "No. Don't worry about me. Get some rest."

"That's—I'm happy to hear it."

"Your new trainer won't be." He shot her a look from the doorway.

"Oh. That." She waved a hand. "I fired him already."

"Well, he needed to learn sometime. How fickle princesses can be."

CHAPTER 6

"*Avoidance*"

TAKES DIFFERENT SHAPES AND FORMS, BUT THE RESULT'S ALWAYS THE SAME.

After a long, sleep-deprived day, Callan finalized his client's report. He sent it to Rayan Wali, CEO of Wali Private Security, and closed his laptop. The late-October sun cast an obnoxious glare through his window. He closed his eyes, hoping to feel the pull of sleep.

Instead, her face floated beneath his eyelids and taunted his brain.

I hope she spoke to HR. Or the cops. As long as she did something. He ran both hands over his face. *Too many women go missing like that.* He sighed.

And then there's you. You swore you'd keep your distance. And that lasted all of, what, a few days? You've gone soft. You have no plan. No escape route. Your position's exposed and your weapon's out of ammunition.

A knock sounded at his door.

I'd never intentionally hurt her. Can't that be enough?

"Hey," Meridian said when he opened the door. She

handed over paper grocery sacks. The smile she gave him was different than last time. Softer.

He nodded and repeated the greeting.

"I hope you're hungry." She slipped past him into his apartment.

"Twenty-four seven."

She flipped her hair off one shoulder. "Once a Marine always a Marine?"

"Semper fi." He placed the bags on the counter. He turned to give her a better greeting, but she'd already moved away.

He frowned. *Something's bothering her.*

Meridian made her way to the oven—long legs covered in dark-colored tights. The tights did nothing to detract from their allure. A short, casual-looking green skirt drew his eyes to the pleasing curve of her hips.

His hunger was different from last time.

She pressed buttons on the oven, then opened and closed the door.

"Steak and potatoes again?" Callan began removing groceries from the bag and placing them on the counter.

"Grilled portobello mushrooms on hamburger buns. For the vegan in you." Meridian grabbed the other bag.

He pulled the Styrofoam-and-cellophane-wrapped steaks out of the bottom of his grocery sack and held them up.

"Now who's a liar?"

Her lips twisted and she looked away. "Nothing says 'thank you for keeping a girl from being date-raped' like steak and potatoes." She plucked the containers from his hands.

"Everything OK at work today?"

"He didn't show. I did speak to HR. It was uncomfortable. I told them my neighbor was a witness. They seem to believe me. But they have to hear his side, too."

"Yeah. There's a process. In the military, could at least have the satisfaction of throwing him in the brig."

"Does sound satisfying about now."

"Hm. Where's my beer?" He peered into the other sack.

She turned and planted a hand on her hip. "Is that how we ask for things?"

He narrowed his eyes. "Did you, by chance, Ms. Daly, bring more delicious ale?" Callan placed a hand on the counter and hovered close; so close, he could lean down and kiss her . . . "I'd sure be grateful."

Meridian ducked around him. She pulled the oversize bottle from the bag and held it out to him. One eyebrow arched. "Was the Southern drawl for my benefit? Or just the only time you've heard someone speak who had manners?"

He brushed his fingers against hers when he drew the bottle from her grip. She blushed and looked away.

"Spent time in the Carolinas." He popped the top from the bottle.

"Oh?"

"Parris Island. Boot camp."

"Ah yes. Marine boot camp." She plunked one seasoned steak into the pan. The meat sizzled; the smell whetted his appetite.

"What was your thing? Your assignment, or—"

"Specialty?"

"Yeah."

He swallowed. Placed the cap back on the bottle. Took a breath. "Sniper."

A small frown. "The guys who camouflage and wait for hours—"

"Sometimes days."

"But then you don't miss, right? At crazy distances, you've calculated all kinds of variables. So you don't miss?"

"I don't have a shot. Lost my line of sight—"

"Take the shot."

"Callan?"

"Hmm? Ah. Yeah. We do our best not to miss." He took a sip of his beer. "Where's yours?"

"I left mine in your fridge. Didn't you notice?"

Callan shrugged and moved to the refrigerator to grab her beer. Another thud from the pan indicated she'd flipped over the steak—to sear the other side.

"So aside from sharpshooting. Geometry, physics, ugh. Your specialty involves stalking and essentially lying in wait. I find this . . . somewhat alarming and oddly telling."

He used his T-shirt to twist off the cap from the lager, and set it on the counter beside her. *She's trying too hard. Avoiding my gaze.*

"You forgot hand-to-hand combat. Reconnaissance. Some medical training. You thinking of joining up?"

"You already told me tiaras aren't part of the uniform. That's a nonstarter."

"Traded ours for JLTVs."

"I have no idea what that is."

"Not-tanks."

"Ah. And w-what did you do before the Marines?"

"High school. Like everyone else."

"Uh-huh." She removed the pan from the burner and wiped her hands off on a paper towel.

"What did you do before princess school?" Callan leaned against the counter and crossed his arms.

"I went to *fairy* princess school," she said, and took a drink of her lager. "Where we learned to flit about in fairy-tales, thank you very much."

There's the Meridian I know. The prissy princess who makes me want to kiss her smart mouth shut.

"High school. College." She used a pair of tongs to move seared pieces of meat from cooking pan to baking pan.

"So, being a fairy princess is an advanced degree."

"And stalkers are apparently Prince Charming–school dropouts." She finally looked at him. Her mouth tucked up on one side; delicate red veins showed in her eyes.

He brushed a piece of hair from her face, intent on stealing a kiss. But before he could try, she gasped and moved away.

"The potatoes. I need to heat them up." She grabbed a container from the counter and flipped it over. "I, uh." She stepped around him. "Yeah. Be right back."

"Uh-huh." He tried to keep from growling.

Meridian moved to the other end of the kitchen, removed the wrapping on the potatoes, and stuffed the container in the microwave.

"I don't stalk you." He sipped his beer. "Yet."

"Very comforting, Brand."

Callan placed the plates of food on the table and moved a chair for Meridian. He sat beside her. The urge to take her hand in his stomped through his brain. She gave him a tight-lipped smile.

"You all right?" He shifted uncomfortably in his seat. *She's here, so it's not like she's avoiding me. But I don't know how to read this . . .*

Meridian looked at her plate, ran a shaky hand over her forehead. "Yeah, just," she said with a sigh, "on edge most of the day." She glanced up but didn't meet his gaze. "I'm better now. Thank you." She touched his arm.

Her warmth suffused from his arm to his shoulder, curling down through his chest. His stomach dispelled the effect with a groan.

They ate in silence. Callan tried to slow his usual pace. *Rapid food inhalation won't impress a fairy princess.*

Meridian cut her food into perfect squares, chewed with a closed mouth, and dabbed at the corners of her lips with her napkin.

"This. It's good. Didn't think they'd teach cooking in fairy-princess school."

"It's actually a very important skill. Not as much magic required when a fairy princess can cook."

"Hmm. Didn't know that."

She pushed a piece of broccoli to the edge of her plate. "There may be a lot you don't know about fairy princesses."

"I think I know this one pretty well." He glanced at his empty dish and sighed. She still had food on her plate.

"Do you?"

Callan grabbed his beer and sat back in his chair. "You tell me."

"What do you really know about me?" Meridian met his gaze. Her eyes gleamed a brilliant shade of bluish green. But she had a tight set to her jaw, and the muscles of her neck strained against her skin.

This, some form of this question—bothered her. It was why she was here.

Callan sucked in a breath. As a sniper, he'd been trained by the Marines to know and recognize *moments*.

Moments when all the training—his focused mind, muscle memory, weapon knowledge . . .

When all the preparation—target reconnaissance, angle of attack, position scouting . . .

When all the setup—hidden amid the terrain, barrel aimed, trajectory known . . .

When everything came together in one crucial moment—when the sniper squeezed the trigger and took his shot.

"I know the woman I see." He straightened in his chair. "Has a smart mouth. A clever sense of humor." He exhaled. His pulse sounded uniform in its rhythm. "A kind heart." She met his gaze. "And tenacious spirit."

He leaned forward and pulled her hand into his. "Which is the nice way of saying she's stubborn as fuck."

"Look who's talking." Meridian pressed her lips together and tilted her head.

"She's patient. A little old-fashioned—in just the *right* way."

She stared at him. Tears collected in the corners of her eyes.

"Do I need some facts and figures to tell me who you are? Or do I have an accurate picture?"

"They clearly don't teach flattery in sniper school."

He tucked a piece of hair behind her ear. "Not a tool we need for the job."

"I guess not." Their fingers tangled together.

"Besides, *my* fairy princess doesn't like empty flattery."

Her eyebrows lifted. "She doesn't?"

"No. She'd rather have genuine respect and admiration."

"Well, true. But not very princessy, when you think about it." She narrowed her eyes and stuck out her chin.

"I won't tell."

"That's not what I meant and you know it."

"So you dropped out of fairy-princess school?"

"Expelled. On a technicality. Didn't make it home before midnight. Lost a pretty expensive shoe."

"A rebellious fairy princess," Callan said with a chuckle. "That I'd believe." A picture of her in a ball gown popped into his mind—with a leather jacket thrown over her shoulders and motorcycle boots peeking out from underneath.

She giggled, and the air in the room lightened. "I like hearing you laugh." Her eyes twinkled.

His entire body reacted to that look. God, he wanted to heft her onto his kitchen table and take her right there. Or at least have her sit in his lap.

"I like you, Callan." Meridian spoke to their joined hands. She lifted her eyes to meet his. "I like being with you."

The uncomfortable feeling surfaced again. His shot taken—it was time to retreat. Except. That wasn't how this mission worked.

"You're the only one who suits me."

He stood from the chair with his plate. There could still be potatoes needing to be consumed.

CALLAN CLEARED THE DISHES FROM THE TABLE AND stacked them in the sink. They'd keep until morning. He held out his hand to help Meridian from her seat. "You don't always have to cook."

"No?" She rose to her feet. "You cook?"

Callan shook his head. "I eat. What I cook isn't for normal humans. But there are places called restaurants." He met her gaze. "I could take you to one. I think you'd like the experience. They cook *for* you."

"That—sounds like a date, Mr. Brand." She crossed her arms. "Or should I refer to you by your rank?"

Callan moved to the den and sat on the sofa. He hoped she would follow him. Maybe this time she'd sit in his lap. Let him hold her again. *Maybe it'll lead to other things, too . . .*

"Sergeant?" Meridian's voice called out after him.

"Lousy guess." He moved closer to the center of the

sofa. Then back to the cushion farthest from the kitchen. "Sergeant is too vague."

"Hmm. I guess Mr. Brand will have to do." Her voice grew nearer. He could make out her darkened reflection in the powered-off monitor. She bit her lip and frowned.

"Hey, come sit down. You need to relax."

She hesitated, then moved to the end of the sofa.

"If you sit down here, I'll give you a shoulder massage. While we finish playing twenty questions."

"Hmm. That sounds, nice, actually."

He patted the front of his couch cushion. Meridian settled in on the floor, between his knees. He moved her hair and ran his thumbs down the back of her neck. She shivered.

"I was a CSO, critical skills operator. Called us Raiders." He watched her reflection as he set to work kneading her trapezius muscles. "I commanded an MSOT, a team, before MARSOC."

"Where did you, um, live?"

"Nowhere for long. Stationed at Camp Pendleton."

"Ah. California."

"Yeah. You grew up in Florida, right? The panhandle?"

"Someone's been internet-searching his neighbors." Her reflection pursed its lips together. He worked his thumbs into rigid spots in her shoulders.

"Can't be too careful." He leaned down to look at her. It made for a nice view. Her chest, at this angle, held a pleasing, rounded shape—in a white thermal shirt, with two buttons undone. She met his gaze.

"I have top-secret clearance. You could be a spy."

Her eyebrows lifted. She straightened. "That sounds far more exciting than being a PR analyst."

"Hmm. I don't want or need exciting. Being normal is difficult enough."

She bowed her head as he kneaded the muscles in her neck. "I don't think you count as normal."

"Should have seen me before. I was a real hardass."

"Was?"

"Hmm." He still wanted to kiss her and shut her up. *I just want to kiss her.*

"So you're all soft and squishy now, is that it?"

Callan let out a puff of air. "No."

"So what do you do now?" She turned around and placed her hand on his knee. "For work, I mean."

"I run a small group of dark-web researchers and threat-intel analysts. My own consulting company."

"Oh! Wow. That's unexpected. It sounds like it's still military-like, though?"

"No rifles."

"Yeah. Seems to be a thing with you. Rifles, I mean."

"We provide targeted data and reporting about cyber threats. It's a niche offering. Something I can do because of my military background and clearance."

"Sounds . . . stressful?"

Callan frowned. *Stressful compared to what?* "It's all relative."

"I—yeah. Stalking's gotta be tough, too."

Callan reached and caught her hand. He towed her forward, then deposited her into his lap. *Finally.*

She smiled; her palm cupped his cheek, and she pressed

her lips to his. Warmth sang from her skin to his. It thrummed through his veins. He opened his mouth and brought one hand up to the back of her neck—urging her closer. He deepened the kiss.

The warm, easy current changed, becoming exciting, electric. Her hip pressed into the tight, aching part of him that wanted to touch more of her skin, to pull her closer. It pleaded its case to his arms, his brain, his lips. *Meridian . . .*

After a few slow heartbeats, she pulled away.

"You changed the subject." Callan eyed her legs and tried not to imagine them straddling his lap. Bare.

"I did? What were we talking about?"

"Me, taking you on a date."

"This isn't a date?" Her fingers traced a path over his left ear. More body parts jumped on the *seduce Meridian* bandwagon.

"I'm fine if it is, but I don't mind taking you out." He met her gaze. "Unless there's a reason you're avoiding the topic."

"No. You seemed like more of a homebody to me. Not in a bad way."

"I am. But you're not as much of one."

She looked away.

"I'd like to"—he tipped her chin in his direction—"do something you'd enjoy."

"Then it's a date. About time you asked me, really. You're not very good at hints." Meridian smiled and rose from his lap.

Wrong direction. "And you're terrible at subtext." Callan stood and caged her in a loose embrace.

"Am I?"

Her citrusy cinnamon scent caught his attention—amplifying his desire. It throbbed and hummed through his veins like a lively melody. "Like this: you should stay for dessert."

"Oh! You didn't strike me as a guy who'd have much of a sweet tooth." She turned in his grip. "But I have some gelato—"

He tightened his arms around her. "Not what I meant."

"You mean"—she fidgeted with the small medallion on his neck—"something else."

Callan remained quiet. Listening.

"Hmm. I have a policy of not sleeping with a guy on the first date."

"It's not our first date." He mentally sighed. He'd have to be content with holding her like this. The melody softened; the sound became sweeter.

"True. It's negative one. We haven't even had our first date."

He frowned at the sharp note. "So, you cooking dinner, us working out together—doesn't count?"

Meridian smiled and pecked his lips. "That. Was incredibly sweet. And endearing." She pulled away.

Wait. Why is she leaving?

"You've been deflecting. Avoiding me. This. Us. Most of the night."

"And yet I was the one knocking on your door." She grabbed her pocketbook and keys from his counter.

Callan beat her to the door. She halted; blond hair

97

formed a curtain in front of her face. "I said you're the only one who suits me, Meridian."

She took a loud, rasping breath.

"It means . . ." He swallowed against a strained feeling in the back of his throat. "What it sounds like."

"It sounds like . . ." Her voice trembled. "Almost like . . ." She looked up; her eyebrows peaked in the midst of her forehead. "A 'till death do us part' type of statement. And that's—"

"Not what you want." The melody quieted. The room fell silent around them.

Her mouth opened, closed. "Not true. I just. It's . . ."

"Scaring you?"

Her fingers traced the logo on top of her small black wallet. "It's thrilling and frightening. But it's—it's too rushed. Too soon. We only . . ." She ran a hand through her hair and leaned back against his door. "This is the first time you've told me anything. About yourself."

"I know."

"Was it intentional? Not telling me? Because it's classified, or your job, or—"

"There are details I can't share. But we were conditioned. To keep information about ourselves, the mission, close." He shoved his hands in his jeans pockets. "It's a bad excuse. But I—" He shrugged his shoulders. "In all fairness, I didn't expect this."

"Didn't expect what?"

"If you were just an acquaintance, it wouldn't matter. Would it?"

"I see. So. I'm supposed to infer that means I'm important to you?"

"It worked."

"I'd prefer to hear you say it. Things like that matter. Hearing the words, that is." She stood on tiptoe and pressed a gentle kiss to his lips.

Callan covered her mouth with his; he pulled her into his embrace. Pressing closer. His lips delivered his message: *I want you to stay.* The melody began again—the notes hitting between sweet and a driving, steady beat.

When a certain part of his anatomy started making demands, he broke the kiss.

"I don't want to avoid you." She lingered in his embrace.

"Good. Now, leave before I get to the point where I can't let you." He took a step back and held his arms down at his sides.

"Can't let me—" Meridian stopped; she blinked. "Ah. Got it." She gave him a quick kiss and rushed out the door.

CHAPTER 7

"Maddening and difficult"

DEFINED THE RELATIONSHIP.

The following Friday night, Callan knocked on her door for a third time. He waited. "Meridian." Adjusted his hold on the bouquet of lilies. Quieted racing thoughts. Breathed. Listened.

No answer.

The rush began again: *Where is she? Is she hurt? Is she angry? Did she forget? How could she forget?*

He banged on her door. His hand shook. Callan tucked his right hand under his left arm and waited for the tremor to subside. "Meridian? Open the door."

Silence.

She hasn't called or texted. Callan leaned back against the wall. He ran a hand through his hair. It trembled. *Dammit, stop. Calm down.*

He sent her a text. Worked to quiet himself. Breathed. Waited.

A grayish-white haze trickled in. Then flowed. He let it

take away the rush. His mind and body stilled. He found his breath, his thoughts disappearing into the fog.

"I'm here, I'm here!" A woman power-walked in long strides around the corner. "I know I'm late, but I got stuck with this stupid project and—"

Callan blinked. She came into focus. *Meridian.* "We have a date."

"Yes, I'm aware. Just." She heaved a sigh and sent him a sharp look. "Give me a few minutes to get changed. You can come in." She squeezed his forearm before unlocking the door.

Her touch dispelled the haze.

"Grab a drink from the fridge while you wait."

Her apartment was the smaller version of his, and mirror-opposite. The living area held a few pieces of wood furniture—a coffee table, a sofa table, a bookcase. Clean surfaces. A few picture frames. He drifted into her residence.

A couple of bottles of his new favorite IPA sat in her fridge. He opened one and moved to the living room. The haze from earlier spun new threads through his mind. He frowned and focused on the cold feeling of the bottle in his hand.

The air and his surroundings sharpened. He sank into Meridian's couch; he liked the colors: a royal blue with maroon and green stripes. The dark wood coffee table rose to the perfect height to rest his boots.

He took a sip of his beer.

The shush of water; pipes groaned. Callan sighed. He launched the app on his phone and moved their reservation back an hour. Thankfully, the restaurant he had chosen still had openings.

A shower. She had to take a—

Fuck. He almost choked on a swallow of beer. His date showered a few feet away. And his brain conjured up the mental image of her: drenched the way she'd been the first time he saw her, but completely nude. Water droplets dotting her skin and clinging to intimate, sensitive places. And little blond curls . . .

Callan stood and started pacing as the rush began again. *Who else has she invited in like this? Doesn't she realize how vulnerable she is?*

Breathe. Pace. Breathe. His mind wandered off.

She lathered soap across her abdomen, working her hands over delicate skin. A light dusting of bubbles trailed behind as her fingers skimmed over the wet, pebbled surface of her breasts.

He measured his steps around the room and counted his breaths. And then a different mental image appeared:

Callan pressed her soaked body against the shower wall. Streams of water beat his shoulders as he bit kisses down her neck to the swell of her breast. Meridian moaned; he slid his hand over the curve of her hip—

Pace. Pace. Breathe. Pace.

The heated apartment air buzzed around him. *Too heavy. It's too heavy to breathe. How long has she been in the shower?* He glanced at his watch. *Five minutes?*

Callan hung his head. He let himself out of her residence and paced measured steps in the hallway. He needed to calm his body, his pulse, his thoughts.

He turned her around and she pressed her back against him. He worked soap over her stomach, then moved lower.

Callan panted and pressed his forehead against the cool window situated between their apartments.

And breathed.

Thirty minutes to shower and change was probably a record for a fairy princess. But not for a former Marine.

Finally, she called out: "Ready." And stepped into the living room.

While Callan hadn't thought she needed to change, he could appreciate the transformation. His *friend* and neighbor had worn business-casual clothes: a long sweater and jeans, with her hair up in a loose clip.

His *date*, however, pulled a piece of her loose, dark-blond hair behind one ear. Her makeup made her eyelashes darker, her eyes rounder. Meridian shrugged one shoulder beneath a loose light-blue sweater. A dark-colored skirt clung to her hips above gray knee-high boots.

Callan wanted to taste her. Instead, he handed her the flowers he'd brought and offered her a smile.

She met his gaze with a grin of her own. *I should just take her back to her shower.* He shoved his hands in his pockets.

"Stargazer lilies? Interesting choice."

He leaned against the wall beside her door. "They looked like you."

"Do you believe flowers have meanings?"

He gestured at himself. "What do you think?" He had dressed up for her, for their date: a button-down shirt and blazer over jeans and his usual work boots. Still a far cry from her *handsome prince*.

A hint of a smile toyed with her lips. "I've always thought you looked like a guy who says what he wants to say —when he wants to say it."

Meridian pulled a vase from her cabinet and ran water into the container. "So, you likely didn't choose red roses on purpose." She unbound the flowers from a clear plastic surround. "But stargazer lilies in dark pink espouse a general optimism. And purity."

"They were on sale."

"You're still a terrible liar." Meridian peered at him around her cabinets. "I know, at least, you weren't a spy."

"General reconnaissance." He crossed his arms. "Not the lying kind of spying."

"The sentiment is very sweet."

The wall to his left attracted his attention. For no partic- ular reason. *Red roses would have scared you off, based on the conversation last week. And yes, I knew you'd try to interpret some meaning from the flowers I chose.*

"You said you were going to take me to this novel place called a restaurant?" She placed the vase in the center of her countertop. The lilies stood tall, the blooms strong and bright. A spicy, exotic fragrance drifted into the air.

"Reconnaissance reports suggest it has all four food groups: steak, potatoes, IPA, and lager."

She laughed. "You're a true romantic, Callan Brand."

"No. But you know what you're getting into."

She folded her arm into his, and he led them out of her apartment.

"And, while we're on the subject: my intentions aren't pure, or whatever."

She met his gaze; her complexion turned a shade brighter than the lilies. "Well, I don't think it meant—"

"I left your apartment while you were showering. You were inviting trouble."

"Maybe I did it on purpose."

His feet stopped moving. "We're going back to your shower."

"OK, OK, I didn't do it on purpose." Meridian tugged him into the elevator. "I'm sorry for tempting you. When you've been"—she smiled—"mostly good to me."

He held her gaze and lifted an eyebrow. "I haven't even started yet."

She gasped. "I'm starting to wonder if you learned *anything* in Prince Charming school." She hurried off the elevator. He took a couple of long strides to catch up with her.

"I was expelled as soon as I arrived on my motorcycle—instead of a white horse."

"Now you're just trying to convince me you're a bad boy."

He opened the exit door and let her go first. A blast of chilled air riffled his collar as they stepped onto the sidewalk. "Did it work?"

She elbowed him in the ribs. "No. Besides, I prefer an emotionally mature man."

He held out his arm; she slipped her gloved hand in the crook of his elbow. "I don't cry. Or wear pink."

Meridian giggled. She leaned into his arm. The sound of her heels clicked on the concrete. "What about getting in touch with your feminine side?"

Callan tilted his head toward her. "No."

Their breaths puffed like clouds as they walked. They caught their rideshare at the curb and climbed into the back seat. "You're just bitter over not getting into princess school."

"Damn right."

THE OUTDOOR SHOPPING AREA BUSTLED WITH PATRONS on a Friday night. Decorated with lights and all the symbols of fall, an autumnal festival served free, appetizing smells to passersby. Callan had chosen a casual Italian place that offered reservations, a quiet ambiance, and a moderate price tag.

Upon arrival, a hostess showed the couple to their table —a booth in a quiet corner. He slipped a twenty into the lady's hand; she smiled, nodded at his date with a grin, and left.

Round fixtures held flameless candles situated in the center of the table. A single orchid plumed from a tiny vase. Callan sat across from her in the cozy restaurant booth. Under the table, his legs stretched at an angle; her boot pressed against the side of his calf.

He liked the small connection. *She's warm, and too inviting.*

No specialty IPA; they chatted back and forth over choosing a bottle of wine. "You like red or white?"

"Red at least has some health benefits. At least, that's what I tell myself."

"I see."

"Are we choosing based on what goes with our dinner, or based on courses or—" she stopped. Bit her lip. Looked up at him. "I like a nice pinot noir?"

He nodded and looked at the list. He read several names and shrugged. "The only thing I know is Oregon makes a good one?"

"They do. But they're not inexpensive."

"You've bought, and cooked me, dinner twice. Not including the pizza."

"But I—"

"You're a modern princess. But your kingdom's currency isn't accepted here. You're stuck letting me pay for dinner."

Her lips curved. "Your consulting business must do pretty well?"

"I can pay my employees and make a reasonable living. Could be more—if I dedicated people to marketing and sales."

Her leg brushed his. She rested clasped hands on the edge of the table.

"Right now, I have all the business I can handle by word of mouth."

"Who knew you were so entrepreneurial?" She lifted

greenish-blue eyes up to meet his gaze. He stared back. Her pink lips formed a subtle pout. That insatiable urge to kiss her started nagging him again.

A small basket of rolls landed on the table in front of them; a waiter wearing a white apron over a tie and shirtsleeves appeared. The man spoke words, but Callan didn't listen. He grunted and gestured at Meridian to convey the message "Ask her."

His date opened her menu and engaged the man in conversation. Callan blinked and the waiter shuffled off toward the back of the restaurant.

"You OK?"

"Hmm?" He glanced across the table. "Yeah. Why?"

"You seem a little distracted."

"Just hungry. And I don't like to fill up on bread."

"I wish I could say the same. About bread. I should add an extra workout day just to burn off the bread calories."

He swallowed the urge to suggest another way to burn calories. But he couldn't hide the smile.

She huffed and rolled her eyes. "Ugh, you and your subtext."

AFTER THE LENGTHY PROCESS OF ORDERING AND pouring wine—their food arrived. Meridian smiled at him over a plate of blackened redfish and sautéed vegetables. "It smells amazing." She took a bite.

"How is it?" Callan cut into the ribeye. It wasn't as red as he liked, but it tasted all right.

"Good. Yours?"

Callan glanced down at his steak and shrugged. "Hm."

"Just 'hm'?"

"My neighbor makes a better one. And she makes house calls."

Meridian's face lit with laughter. "Don't get used to it."

"Too late."

"Hmmmm." She turned her head to give him a sidelong glance that made his body tighten all over again. The phantom image of her wearing nothing but soap floated around in his head.

Callan motioned at her plate. "I don't always have to eat steak and potatoes."

Meridian nodded her head a bit too much. "Very convincing. Considering." She pointed at his plate of steak. With potatoes—and green beans.

"I just meant: we can eat things you like." He studied his plate. "Isn't that what couples do? Compromise?"

"Couples?" Her voice pitched like the word was a surprise.

His insides grumbled, and not because he was still hungry. He scowled. "We've discussed this."

"I'm not sure. Have we?"

He straightened in his seat. "You're avoiding again. Or playing a game. And you're not like the women who play games." *Or I wouldn't bother*.

"You could ask me." Blue-green eyes sparked in the overhead light.

"Ask you to—" He shook his head. "Be my girlfriend? Be exclusive? What do you need me to say, *Meridian*?"

"Either of those would have been fine." She picked the napkin out of her lap. "Without the attitude. *Callan.*" She slapped it on the table and stood.

"I didn't mean to give you attitude." He placed a hand on top of hers. "We just discussed this a week ago. I told you what I meant."

She sat back down.

"If my message isn't received, tell me what I need to say."

"I don't want to," she said to her plate, "date anyone else. But I—I'm not sure."

"Of what?"

"I'm not sure how serious." Her eyebrows pinched together. "I mean, I know you're not asking right now or anything. But I'm not sure I'm ready to get married—as an example. And I—I want to be sure we're on the same timetable."

His princess was turning out to be *complicated.* "This is enough for now."

"This? Food and kisses and working out?"

His heart knocked against his ribcage. "No, not like that."

"Which part needs to change? Because over the past few weeks, this"—she waved her fork at the space between them—"isn't enough for me, either."

"I can do more for you." He returned to cutting his steak in a slowed-down version of eating.

"I want to go out places. Bring you with me to meet friends."

Callan nodded. "I can do that."

"What about parents? Family?"

He straightened his shoulders and met her gaze. "Within mission parameters."

"Plus-one at a wedding." She arched an eyebrow.

"Acceptable."

"All right. And although I'm sure I can guess . . ." Her head tilted. "What's missing from your side?"

"Watching sports." He took a bite of green beans and chewed.

Her mouth opened and closed. "What?"

"Did you expect me to say *sex*, Meridian?"

"Yes."

"You have a one-track mind." He swallowed a smile. *She's too easy to rile up.*

"Me?" Red tinged her cheeks. "You're mister subtext."

"If sex is that important—"

"Ha ha, Mr. Brand. Very clever."

"I'm a physical person." He placed his napkin on the table. "We started off working out together. I'd like that to continue."

"It's"—she nodded—"on the table."

"I don't mean here. That's not what restaurants are for."

"You're absolutely awful sometimes! I mean—!" She heaved a sigh. "You know what I mean."

He grinned. "You turn pink when you're angry."

"If there's nothing chocolate on the menu, you're taking me someplace else for dessert." Meridian pointed at him. "And not my shower!"

112

CHAPTER 7

C<small>ALLAN PINNED</small> M<small>ERIDIAN BENEATH HIM ON HER</small>
couch—her breathy moans loosening ties on his strict discipline and control. He kissed a path down her neck. Her
fingers dug into the space between his shoulder blades. He
pushed fabric out of the way to get to the soft skin of her
breast.

He settled more of his weight into her.

"Ah, Callan . . ."

His name on her lips. Her hot breath against his ear. He
laved his tongue over the peak of her breast. His left hand
palmed the other and applied gentle pressure. *She feels so
good . . .*

"C-Callan." She pushed against his shoulders. "Uhhhn.
N-not yet. Please."

He closed his mouth to keep the deep sigh and pathetic
whimper caged inside. He pushed himself into a sitting
position.

"I—I . . ." Meridian pulled her sweater down and sat up.
She combed fingers through her hair.

"It's fine. Not on the first date." He stood from the
couch.

"It's not that. I mean it is, but—it's more than that."

"OK." He set his jaw.

"I, uh, need to tell you something. A couple of some-
things. Actually." She folded her hands in her lap.

"Sure."

"One of the reasons why my dates in college weren't
what I considered boyfriends"—she twisted her fingers
together—"is because I—I dunno, after Jase . . . I just felt

like it was a mistake to have slept with him. To have been intimate with someone else, who didn't feel the same way."

Callan nodded. "Understood. As I said before, I'm a physical person, so it's something I want. But I won't pressure you if you're not ready."

"I trust you." She stood up, and took his hand into hers. "There's something else. My family . . . They're a bit of a challenge."

He knew what she was going to say. The closed-adoption search hadn't yielded much information—other than her birth father's family name. And that Meridian hadn't been in contact with the family for around a decade.

"I was adopted. I didn't find out until I was around twelve, after my father—my adoptive father, that is—died. There was a lot of mess and confusion. The short version is: Meridian Daly isn't my legal name. Anymore."

"I'm aware."

She blinked. "You're what?"

"It's what I do for a living."

She dropped his hand and gaped at him. "That's more than an internet search, *Callan*."

"I wasn't kidding about my security clearance." He stuffed his hands in his pockets. "I research everyone who lives in our building."

"You know everyone—"

"I helped the police find a missing kid. The leasing lady pretends to look the other way whenever I stop in."

A sharp intake of breath. "So you did a search before we met."

"I dug deeper afterward. The DOD will conduct an official investigation on all members of my household."

"So, you're saying . . ." Meridian blinked. "I'd have to pass a background check. Once we were, *if* we were." She frowned. "Serious."

Anger flared through his system. "This is *serious*, or I wouldn't bother."

"I—well. From now on, if you want to know something, ask me. If there's a background check I need to pass, to be part of your life, I should at least know about it. Agreed?"

Callan nodded. But the rage still swirled beneath the surface of his skin.

"So then, you already know—about my birth family?"

"The name. Was there something else?"

"Well. No? Just." She sat back down on her couch. "The Cavalliers happen to be . . ." Meridian smoothed hands over her skirt. One thumb lingered on her inner thigh. His anger notched itself down several degrees. "Let's see, how do I put this? Arrogant. Small-minded."

"So they're wealthy."

"Intrusive. Controlling."

"Sounds like perfect casting for an evil stepmother. To a princess."

She huffed and glared. "They're not *evil*. Just. I went from one extreme to the other. My adoptive father could never make time for me. So at first, the Cavalliers' interest was . . . I dunno. They seemed to care. Then I realized they only cared about their family name and how things *appeared*. I just wanted nothing to do with it. Or them. I was a dumb, rebellious kid. And I made some real mistakes."

"Your mother?"

"Yeah. She was really angry when I changed my name. I wish I hadn't."

"Which is why you're going by Daly now?"

"I don't feel like I have the right to change it back. He wasn't my father."

"Well, sounds like he didn't measure up to your definition of one."

"What's that supposed to mean?"

"Family's tough. Everyone forms a picture of what it's supposed to be, somewhere along the way. A definition. A set of expectations. Maybe he never wanted to be a father, but he was making your mom happy. Or maybe he thought the best way to be a dad was to provide for you and her. You don't know his story."

"I never got the chance to ask."

"The Corps is the only family I have. Guys like Watts." He blew out a breath. "Stuck with him the same as any brother. Or sister, with all that ridiculous hair."

She pressed her lips together, but couldn't hold back a smile.

"There's a saying we have: It's not about blood. It's the sweat and tears that makes us family."

"I'm going to write a letter to the—who's the head of the Marines?"

"The Commandant?"

"That guy. I'm going to tell him that he's missing out on a side hustle selling greeting cards written by hardass Raiders. I can picture them in stationery aisles, with your soft and squishy sayings on one side, your sniper insignia on the back."

"That bratty mouth's gonna get you in trouble one of these days."

"With whom?"

"Me. First I'm going to kiss you so hard you have no choice but to shut up. Then I'll make you open those lips again, but only to scream my name."

"What? Y-you're the—"

He cut off her protest with a kiss. Tentative lips met his; he seized the advantage, cradling the back of her head as he trapped her against him. Her body, against his; the temperature of the air in her apartment ratcheted up. He wrapped his arm around her waist, and slid his palm over her rear. Fingers slipped through his hair. She bit at his lower lip, then swept her tongue against his.

He broke the kiss. "You have a rule about first dates."

"Yeah," she huffed. Her eyes gleamed beneath long dark lashes.

Such a brat. "It's almost midnight. I should go. Before one of us turns into a pumpkin."

"I'm surprised you know that reference."

"Princess-school entrance exams."

"Right." Meridian walked him to the door. "For the record. Prince Charming doesn't kiss like that."

"He's doing it wrong."

"I agree. The Marine Corps has better technique."

"That's not the Corps."

"Oh no?" She drew her hand down the side of his cheek.

"What would convince you I'm serious enough . . ."

"To let you stay, you mean?"

"We could elope."

She dropped her hand. "What? Elope? It'll take you more than one date, Brand." She pushed him away.

"Tomorrow?"

"Go!" She opened the door. He stepped into the hall-way, then turned and leaned down. She pecked his lips. "You're the brat," she said. "But I had a wonderful time on our first date."

He nodded. "Good night, princess."

Before letting himself into his apartment, Callan turned around. Meridian's door clicked shut.

I know you think we're too different. I see it on your face when you say things like "if" we decide we're serious. He sighed. *I'm the hardheaded grunt who'd go to hell and back for you. The trick'll be not taking you with me on the journey.*

CHAPTER 8

"Connection"

WAS THERE A TIME WHEN IT WASN'T SO DIFFICULT?

Not long after negotiating the terms of their relationship, Meridian's friend Nora invited the couple to join her and her new boyfriend for drinks. And a few rounds of pool.

Callan inwardly groaned at the invite, but tried to appear enthusiastic. Or at least like he hadn't just been quarter-decked.

The restaurant and bar reminded Callan of a city's version of a honky-tonk. It wasn't the type of place Callan would take a princess, but she appeared happy enough to be there.

I'll pass on the food. Callan eyed the list of beers on tap. He couldn't help scouting the environment out of the corner of his eye.

Three guys in leather biker jackets hovered over a pool table. *No name on the back, so not gang members.* A group of frat boys surrounded a separate table, a few over from the bikers. One smacked a waitress on the ass as she walked by.

"So how'd you get him to come out of his foxhole?" Watts pointed the tip of his beer bottle in Callan's direction. The walking pain-in-the-neck grinned.

"Grey." Nora's voice sounded like a warning. The dark-haired girl jabbed an elbow into her boyfriend's ribcage. She mouthed, "Sorry, Mare," across the table.

"It took quite a lot." Meridian gave him a sidelong glance—a smile playing on her lips. His entire body reacted to that look.

"I bet."

"It didn't. I just asked him." Her hand found his under the table.

"He never says yes when I ask him." Watts threw his hands in the air and shook his head.

"She's better-looking."

The mechanic laughed. "Not gonna argue that." He raised his bottle in a small salute.

Callan relaxed into the cushion of the booth. Their table sat along the front wall of the restaurant. A large picture window over his left shoulder looked out into the parking lot. At this time of day, the glass made for a better mirror than a window.

Their waitress brought and distributed drinks.

"Did he ever tell you what a daredevil he was in the Corps?"

Nora leaned over and muttered something in Watts's ear. It didn't matter; the gregarious oaf would do as he pleased. And what pleased his *friend* most involved trying to get under Callan's skin.

Like the annoying little brother he'd never wanted.

"Daredevil? I guess that's not *too* surprising, but you don't strike me as an adrenaline junkie." Meridian met his gaze. He stared at his pint glass. His shoulders tightened. He took a deep breath. *Don't let him get to you. Don't let them see. Just breathe. Don't remember.*

"First out of the plane every time."

Nora's head whipped around to stare at him. "Paratrooper?"

He pulled his hand from Meridian's grip and continued his breathing.

"HAHO exercises. We all were. Had to be." Watts placed an arm around Nora's shoulder. "But this guy." A sly smile. "Did you tell her about the time your main chute didn't deploy?"

"No, Watts." Every muscle in his neck and shoulders hardened. "It's not—"

"You're supposed to slow your ass down." The mechanic talked with his hands and his beer bottle. "Become as horizontal as you can, give yourself time to deploy your reserve chute." Dark-brown eyebrows drew into a frown above a wide grin. "But not this guy."

"What'd he do?" Nora gasped. She stared at Callan like he was a fish in an aquarium.

"He beelines for the ground. Just takes some hard left turn at Albuquerque or some shit, and opens his reserve chute inches before hitting sixteen hundred feet. The whole squad figured we were just gonna find his carcass."

Wind whipped through him. Cold air thrashed at his goggles, his fatigues, his pack; it ripped down his back.

"But aside from a broken bone, dude was fine.

Grumpier than shit, but too stubborn to die. Even finished the mission. If you can believe that."

Callan ignored the looks he could see in the reflection of the window. He took a halting breath and told his body to relax. *It's just a story. It's in the past. Don't picture it. Don't remember.*

But his memory was a terrible place . . .

He fought a dark terror that made his whole body burn. No time. No time to panic. No time to feel.

Focus.

Focus or you're gonna fuckin' die!

Meridian's hand on his elbow. "Callan?"

He drew in a ragged breath. "I was repositioning."

"I'm just glad you're here." She leaned over to give him a kiss; he turned so that it landed on his cheek. She frowned.

"I needed a softer landing with the reserve chute, or, possibly, no chute." He tucked his hands under his legs. "There was a marshy area three clicks north of our intended target."

"Don't let him fool you, princess. He's as hard-core as they come."

"All right, well, I think you've told on him enough." Nora's voice. The groan and squeal of movement across vinyl seats. "Let's go see if that old junker of a jukebox over there works, lover boy."

Callan stared at the window and worked on finding his breath.

"Sounds good! I want to buy that thing. It looks awesome!" Watts's loud voice grated on Callan's eardrums.

Then, a little bit softer as they walked away: "I was

trying to help. The girls can't take their panties off fast enough after a story like that."

"Greyson." Nora hugged his arm and giggled.

"Heh. It worked with you."

Meridian placed a hand on Callan's arm. He tried not to jump out of his skin.

"What's wrong?" She peered up at him.

He glanced at her out of the side of his eye. "Nothing."

"Or maybe I should ask you how many girls have taken their panties off for you after that story."

Deep breath. Hold. Exhale. He shivered. *When did the air turn so cold?* "Not many."

"So, there have been some?" She fiddled with her napkin on top of the table. Bending one corner, then turning it to bend another.

"What do you want to know? The number of girl-friends? Whom I've slept with? Or something else?"

"I just—I want to know more about you."

"Isn't it enough to know who I am now?"

"It's a way that people connect. Sharing past experiences? I know you were shut away in the Marines for some time, but certainly you haven't forgotten that?"

"And what past experiences could *you and I* have in common?"

"I dunno. A first date? A first love." She shrugged. "Graduation. A school dance?"

Callan pressed his eyes closed and willed his hands to stop shaking.

"Sports?" Meridian grabbed his chin. His eyes snapped open. "There have been a number of studies that demonstrate that what humans strive for, our needs, are remarkably similar across cultures and other boundaries. I don't see *you and me* as so different."

"You always have," Callan said with a sigh, "so many words I don't." He put his arm around her and kissed her forehead.

"Hmm. We have ways of making you talk." Meridian snuggled into his embrace. She warmed him. His shoulders released some of the tightness.

"Does it involve removing your panties?"

"Ha ha. How about they won't come off until you talk."

"I've withstood greater tortures." Loud, screaming death-metal music erupted from the overhead speakers. He groaned. "They got the jukebox to work."

"Good! I'll go check it out." She disentangled herself, gave him a quick kiss, and hopped to her feet. Her warmth receded.

"Meridian."

She pivoted to face him. Eyes bright, she met his gaze and smiled. "Yes?"

"He'll tell you more stories. I wonder if that still counts as shared experiences." He met her gaze over the tilt of his pint glass.

She pursed her lips together and lifted an eyebrow.

He glanced away. "Let me know."

Callan remained behind in the booth. Meridian moved toward the pool table Watts and Nora had rented. The death-metal song his friend always looked for on a jukebox —no one knew why—finished playing.

He watched the trio of friends from across the restaurant. He knew they wouldn't necessarily talk about him, but after the story Watts had just told . . .

The beer tasted warm, almost sour. Watts and Meridian broke away—to hover near the jukebox. The table of preppy guys noticed Nora.

Time to move.

He stood from the table and crossed the dining area to the game room. He took up a position at the end of the pool table, and shot his worst glare at the guys hitting on his buddy's girl. A couple of elbows, some muttering, and the trio of idiots wandered back to their game.

Callan crossed his arms and sat back against the felt table. Since Watts and Meridian were standing three-quarters turned his direction, he had a decent view of their faces. And happened to be an excellent lip-reader.

". . . difficult one to get to know."

"It's been a process. Every other guy I've met who was interested managed to ask me out within the first couple of weeks of our acquaintance." She tucked a piece of hair behind her ear. "Callan took—hmm, almost five months? After getting over himself and that hardass Marine thing he does. I thought he hated me."

"It's part of his charm. No, not really. You're already a candidate for sainthood somewhere." Watts shook his head and swigged his beer.

"I cooked him dinner in his apartment on a Friday night. Still, nothing."

Callan smiled. *Not nothing. I got the hint.*

"He's cautious. And has reasons for everything he does." Watts's beer hovered over his lips, and Callan missed some of what he said. ". . . analysis has, at times, bordered on obsession. He's damned good at anything he wants to be good at."

"I can see that."

Don't say 'except for relationships,' or I will beat you.

"And the kind of sonofabitch who'd lay his life down for ya. For all the wrong reasons. A damned good brother—in the Marine sense."

Her mouth curved up, but it didn't reach her eyes. "I can see that, too."

"No, you don't get it." Watts slapped his beer down on top of the jukebox as he leaned into her personal space. "Great Marine, lousy friend. A real shit."

This is his idea of good *behavior. He's done enough damage for one day.* He moved toward the two friends.

Meridian shook her head. "You care more . . ." She turned away.

"You're going to have to be tenacious."

"Like you?" A soft smile lit her eyes.

"Damned right."

Callan paused—within earshot now.

"He's got a kindness." Meridian spoke to the jukebox, her fingers splayed over the plexiglass dome. Her tone held a wistful timbre. It reminded Callan of the way people spoke at funerals. He moved behind Watts.

"Even when he griped at me to be cautious about people, I could tell. He meant—he meant to care for me." She tossed her hair over one shoulder as she glanced up. "I won't pretend he's an easy one to deal with all the time. But. Something in me feels like . . . he's worth it."

Air squeezed from his lungs, and his head felt light.

"Glad somebody thinks so."

Callan grabbed Watts's shoulder; he drilled his fingers into the trapezius muscle at the base of his friend's neck. "You should've been able to tell I was standing here."

"Ow! Shit! That fuckin' hurts, jackass." The mechanic whirled around.

"Nora's been alone for five minutes and already has other guys hitting on her. You'd better go."

"Oh, this'll be fun." Watts made a fist and cracked his knuckles.

"Don't stir up trouble, dick," Callan called out after him. "I won't back you up this time."

"That's what you said last time, too." He bounded off in the direction of the pool tables.

"I meant it then!" He grumbled at Meridian, "This is why I say no when he asks."

"Stealth and blending in. You're still a stalker."

"Find out what you needed to know?"

"I already knew everything I needed to. Did you discover something interesting?" She tilted her head. Aquamarine eyes glittered in the dim lighting.

"Nothing I didn't already know."

"I'd need the skills of a super spy to surprise you, wouldn't I?" She leaned closer; he liked the way she fit against him.

He shrugged.

"Anything else?"

"I thought this was about shared life experiences, not my many flaws."

She moved to face him. "Have you"—Meridian trailed her fingers from his elbows to grasp his hands—"let yourself experience life? I get the feeling that you watch, wait, even calculate. But the times you're *in the moment* are few and far between." She appeared to study him.

"How about we play the game with our friends?"

"Now who's avoiding?"

He brought his hand up to her cheek. "I was answering the question." He wrapped his arm around her waist. Her citrusy cinnamon scent drifted up and caught his attention. *I don't always have the words. But you're worth it, to me, too.*

"Then . . ." she murmured. Her palms came to rest on his chest. "What you're saying is . . . I may or may not be correct, but—" She met his gaze. A tender smile. Her soothing warmth. "Right now, you want to—" Her breath hitched. "Be here. With me and our friends?" Her eyes drifted closed.

Callan covered her mouth with his.

CALLAN WALKED HER TO HER DOOR, HER HAND TUCKED between his elbow and ribcage. A comfortable quiet had settled between them during the drive back to their apartment building. Comfortable, except for wanting to touch her. In that perfect, bare space between the top of her knee and the bottom of her skirt.

She looked at him, her back to her apartment door. "Come in? And talk?" Meridian's eyelashes formed a seductive fringe around her eyes.

He leaned close. "Just talk?"

"Just talk." She gave him a sidelong glance with a half smile. Her complexion flushed and her eyes sparkled.

"Sure." He stifled the groan that wouldn't earn him any Prince Charming points. *How long will she make me wait?*

She closed the door and started toward the kitchen. "Coffee?"

"Water's fine." He sat down.

Meridian placed a water bottle on the coffee table and sat next to him. She settled her head on his shoulder. "You seemed a little distant tonight. Your friend's story bothered you."

The muscles in his neck stiffened.

"You know, your past," she said, and tilted her head to look up at him. "It doesn't change anything."

He nodded, and escaped by leaning forward to grab the bottle of water. *Don't ask.*

She soothed her fingers through the hair on the back of his head. "You don't talk about your family. Outside of what you've said about the Marines. They're like family to you."

He pressed his eyes closed and focused on her ministrations. Tiny shivers coursed through the muscles of his back. *I don't want to think about it.* "Just the Corps."

Her fingers paused. "Callan?" She pulled on his chin.

"Don't."

Meridian kissed him, then. Her mouth at first sweetness and syrup. She drew him in. The tension seeped from his muscles and oozed from his pores. He broke away, took a breath, and renewed the fervor of their kiss. Hungry, she devoured his lips. He slipped his tongue into her mouth.

That heated haze began to unfurl—growing, longing. It nudged his heart rate up to a sprint. He wrapped an arm around her waist, and pulled her into his lap. Her heated gaze held his. Gentle fingers stroked the side of his face.

She smiled. Tenderness lit her eyes. Part of him wanted to live in that look, to have her always look at him that way. But the unfurling heat; it wanted to bite and suck it off her features—until she could only stare at him with pulsing, raging desire. His stomach flipped over; he maneuvered her down onto the couch.

He kissed her again, deep and slow—feeling the warmth of her arms around him. The sweet agony of her, pliant and affected, moaning beneath him. He broke the kiss. "You just wanted to talk."

"You're complaining?"

"No." He leaned down, into her—kissing her neck, licking and sucking available flesh. A soft gasp escaped her lips. He ran his hand over her stomach to her ribcage. His thumb stroked the curve of her breast. "I won't go too far." He brushed his fingers over the peak of her chest. He found the nipple and rubbed circles into the light fabric of her bra. It tightened into a pebble; he wanted to find it with his teeth.

"I'm not—" She took a seething breath. He stilled. "I'm . . . I'm sorry."

"It's all right." He bit a harsh kiss into her neck and sat up. "I'll get those panties off you someday."

"Callan!" She bolted upright, adjusting her bra beneath her sweater. Her hair mussed, lipstick smeared. Meridian ran a finger over the side of her mouth.

He wanted to lick the rest of her makeup off. "I should go." He stood, and covertly adjusted that aching part of his anatomy.

"Mmmm?"

He glanced at her. He felt rough and raw, and his body hurt. She glowed.

"I guess you should. But I had a nice time with you." Her gaze locked with his. Blue-green eyes glittered.

"Thanks for the talk."

"Ha ha." She rose from the couch and leaned into him. "Maybe if you talked a bit more, I wouldn't have to resort to such tactics."

"I'll never say another word."

She raised an eyebrow. "Sounds like a challenge."

"It is." He pulled her into a loose embrace.

Meridian rolled her eyes before settling her head on his chest.

"But you should know. I've been through SERE training."

"SERE?"

"Survival, evasion, resistance—to interrogation—and escape."

Meridian pulled from the circle of his arms. "I have no doubt." Her tone sobered. "You could evade, resist, or escape, if you chose. And you'd survive just fine."

He straightened his shoulders. *What is she saying?*

"But I wonder if survival is enough."

An invisible hand grabbed him around his ribcage and squeezed. Hard. He turned away. Opened the door.

"Callan?" Her voice caught him around the throat. He

tried to swallow and couldn't. He leaned his forehead against the edge of the door. Could he leave and not answer? Would she accept that?

No, she's made it clear, she's waiting for me to tell her . . . too many things. Things that hurt. Things I don't want to say. Walking away is the same as giving up. And if there's one thing I know, once I stop trying—whether she stays a day, a month, or a year longer, it doesn't really matter. The end result is the same.

He gripped the doorknob, stood his ground, and gave it everything he had. "It's not. Anymore." He ducked his head and stepped into the hall. He shut the door behind him.

I don't know how to say what you want me to say. But I won't stop trying.

CHAPTER 9
"Undone"

A LACK OF CONTROL IS A LACK OF DISCIPLINE.

Callan slung his arm around Meridian's shoulder, steering her toward his apartment as they reached the top of the stairs. They'd spent a random evening at the indoor batting cages. Surprisingly, his princess knew how to hit softballs. Even softballs thrown for speed.

She let him help with her stance. Hands steadying her hips, slipping over her thighs to her knees. A surreptitious kiss against the back of her neck—earning him a glare and accusation that he was distracting her on purpose.

The best part of the evening. So far.

They reached his door; Meridian pulled on his arm, and kissed his earlobe. Her breath puffed against his ear as two soft, silken lips caressed a surprisingly sensitive part of his body. As she started to pull away, her teeth bit down—sending a shock wave through his system.

He threw his shoulder into the door as he grabbed Meridian, swinging her around his body to deposit her in his apartment. "You're starting something," he said in a rough voice. He shut his door and turned the deadbolt.

Her eyes wide, she gave him an innocent smile. "Am I?"

"You know you are." He brought his hands up to cup her face and settled his mouth over hers. She kissed back with a fervor that began his undoing. He pushed her against the door, and bit kisses into the flesh of her neck.

"Mmmm." Her arms hooked under his shoulders and held him in place.

He paused. His lips hovered above her mouth. They'd had this conversation, more than a few times, over the past few weeks. He'd promised to take their relationship slow, let her dictate the speed of their commitment—physical, emotional, and the place where the two intersected. He just asked her to be clear about her expectations.

"Honest answer."

"Not yet. I—I just—" She met his gaze; her mouth turned down, her eyebrows pinched.

He swallowed the sigh; he'd promised her under-standing and patience. His body had waited out worse. "Proceeding with alternate mission objective." He hauled her against him and picked her feet up off the floor. He carried her into his bedroom and set her down.

That hand on her hip. The sassy purse of her lips. His princess exuded attitude like she commanded an entire battalion. "This doesn't feel like—"

He caught her free hand and pulled it to his mouth. He pressed a kiss to each of her fingertips. "I won't cross the line."

"Then what's this alternate mission objective?"

He leaned forward and spoke next to her ear. "Recon-naissance." He toyed with the hem of her blouse.

One eyebrow arched.

"Stripping you naked." He yanked the shirt over her head—revealing her bra and the tan skin of her abdomen.

She crossed her arms against her chest. "What? B-but!" She took a step back, but had nowhere to go but his bed. Her skin pricked into goosebumps along her forearms.

"I need to determine my primary position." He placed his hands on her hips and met her gaze.

"Primary position?"

"Angle of attack. For when you *are* ready."

"I'm not the enemy."

He kissed her cheek. Her earlobe. Licked the sensitive spot right behind her ear that made her shiver. "Can't I see? All of you, Meridian?" He tipped her head to look at him.

She narrowed her eyes as she slid her arms around his neck. "Only if *you're* going to take it all off, Mr. Marine."

He grinned as he pulled her hands away from his neck. "Be careful what you ask for." He ripped his T-shirt over his head. She returned her hands to his chest, running them over his abdomen and up to his shoulders. Her touch thrilled through his veins, and aroused the ardor of inter-ested parts of his body. But she was throwing gasoline on a fire she wasn't going to let live and burn.

She wants me. So why is she holding back? He kicked off his shoes and unbuttoned his pants, shedding his jeans. His arousal tented the fabric of his boxers.

Meridian, in her bra, skirt, and shoes, backed away.

"Where are you going?" He grabbed her around the waist. "You did ask."

"I did." She nodded. "And I stand by. My request." Her teeth bit into her bottom lip.

"I think I turn you on."

Sparkling eyes. Flushed cheeks. "Not in the slightest. Whatever gave you that idea?"

"The way you're looking at me."

"And how . . . am I looking at you?"

He moved pieces of her hair over her shoulder. "Hungrier than I look at that IPA you bring over. Worse than the steak."

"I promise." Her gaze met his. A flash of heat roiled through him. He tamped it down. "You're more than a piece of meat to me, Callan."

"You can start by using me. I'll win you over in the end," he whispered against her lips.

She rolled her eyes. "You're terr—"

He cut her off with a kiss. She moved her mouth against his for a brief moment before breaking away. Her chest heaved.

"You're still wearing too much." He pulled her against him. A short, audible breath left her lips. He unhooked her bra, slipping the straps from her shoulders and tossing it aside; his erection lurched when she pressed her bare breasts against his chest. He seized her mouth into another kiss.

He maneuvered her onto the bed, then pulled off her shoes before settling beside her. She lay there, her hair pooled above her head, drenching his pillow; the moonlight from his bedroom window painted silver streaks with its glow.

Her breasts formed full, pink-tipped mounds. She had been generous about letting him touch and tease—and even taste. But the bra had never come all the way off. And the more sensitive and heated part of her body had been almost completely off-limits. Eventually, he wanted to *know* every inch of her. Tonight, he'd be satisfied to look at her.

He ran a finger along the waistband of her skirt. Aqua eyes met his. "You're still wearing clothes."

"If I take off my boxers, the rest of your clothing comes off."

She sat up. "And then what?"

"Just sleep. Beside me. That's enough for now. If you're OK with it."

"Won't that be hard—"

He arched an eyebrow.

"Difficult?"

Callan took a deep breath. Exhaled. "Yes."

"And you still . . . are all right with that?"

"Yes."

"Can I," she said with a tilt of her head, "touch you? Him?"

"If you want. But I still want to see how beautiful you are."

Meridian rose to a kneeling position on the bed, her face crimson even in the muted lighting. She hooked her thumbs in the elastic beneath her navel, and then moved them to her hips. She pulled the last of her clothing from her body, and tossed it to the floor. She held his gaze for a moment.

He gave her a small smile, and she stretched out beside him —completely nude.

The moonlight caressed her neck and her ample, pert breasts, her nipples puckered into little oval-shaped pebbles. The windowpane cast a diagonal shadow across her stomach. Slim hips framed a small thatch of blond curls just above the junction between her legs. Silver light tangled in the mess of hair; it illuminated the skin of her long, well-shaped thighs.

He wanted to memorize every detail. Wished she'd let him touch her, taste her, help her enjoy the physical act of joining their bodies. He rolled onto his side. Propped his head up on one hand. Her legs shifted and she squirmed.

"Are you uncomfortable?"

She turned her head and met his gaze. "A little cold."

"So I see." He pressed a kiss to her shoulder to hide his grin.

"Ha ha."

"You look like you might bolt for the door."

An arm drifted up to cover her chest.

"There's nothing to be embarrassed about." He skimmed his knuckles over the curve of her hip. "Your body; you seem comfortable enough most of the time. Why is this different?" He brushed his thumb against the gooseflesh at her waist.

"Because you can see everything. The imperfections—" Her toes contracted and released; one foot covered the other.

"You're beautiful, Meridian."

"So . . ." She lifted off the mattress and placed her hand on his cheek. "So are you."

His breath hitched.

"But you're cheating." Her fingers danced along the waistband of his shorts. "Your boxers need to come off."

Callan struggled to take a breath. He needed to breathe. She tugged on his shorts, pulling them down his legs. He tensed all over. Gasped for air.

And then her fingers brushed his length. Callan about leapt off the bed. "Meridian . . ."

"Is—is it too much? I don't want to . . . torture you. I just, well, I think he likes me."

Her touch electrified his entire body, binding his lungs and starving his brain of oxygen. He maneuvered her hand around his shaft and demonstrated the motion he wanted. Once, twice, then he released her.

Meridian worked her hand up and down in a slow, sliding motion. Callan sucked in rasping breaths, his control crumbling like it had already burnt to ash. He thrust against her palm. She increased the speed of her strokes; he groaned and moved with her.

He opened his eyes and reached for her, pulling her down for a kiss. Her tongue darted into his mouth and teased against his. Raw. Fevered. She broke away, still maintaining her pace. His own fluid slicked her hand and lubricated the effort.

"What. Are you doing," he gritted out between clenched teeth. His body surged and fell to her rhythm.

"Is it not good?"

"Uhhhhn," Callan moaned and choked—trying to breathe. Every muscle in his body tightened. Hardened.

"Be here. In the moment, with me." Her voice seared through him. Her hot breath curled into his ear.

If she bites again, I'm going to cum.

"What will it take? To get you to let go?"

He closed his eyes. All of him focused in one space. Hazy. Blurred. He couldn't fight it. "You're. One. To. Talk."

"But I'm trying to help. It has to hurt. To wait. But you do. And I want—"

Her tongue swirled over the tip of his erection. His eyes shot open and his body snapped in half. Her lips parted, taking a couple of inches into her mouth. *Dear God, she may kill me.* A few thrusts and he had to grab her, pull her away.

Callan sat up, turned his back to her; he grabbed his cock, pumped it a few times, and finished in his hand.

Air, beautiful air, filled his lungs again. Bent forward, he heaved, gulping large breaths. Her hands found his shoulders; his skin felt as though several layers had peeled off.

"Are you OK?"

No. You almost caused me to lose my breath. My control. And I promised you . . .

"Good," he lied. He used his discarded T-shirt to clean up.

"Just good?"

He clenched his eyelids shut. "You like to live dangerously."

"Are you dangerous to me?"

"When you do that." He turned to face her. "Yeah."

Warm, tender eyes met his. "Did it help, though? Can I stay? Without torturing you?"

"I told you I'd be fine."

"But you hold so much back. Away from me. I want . . ." She wrapped her arms around him. "I want all of you, too." She nuzzled the back of his neck. "I want you to be here with me. Not somewhere else."

He took a deep, calming breath before moving back onto the bed. He folded her against him; his skin simmered every place she touched. Her arm draped across his ribcage and one calf slid over his shin.

She lifted her head and looked at him through lowered lashes. "Tell me. Tell me something you *feel*."

His mouth opened and closed. Feel? How did he feel? People didn't ask him that. Feelings, in his experience, were volatile. Detrimental. Something to be pushed aside. Managed. Contained. Ignored. And that was the problem. With this. Her. Anyone who wanted to be close.

He could touch her. He could enjoy and even do his best to please her. But she'd told him, from the beginning, she wanted something more. A sense of intimacy, shared between lovers.

I don't know how to give her that.

Callan pressed his eyes closed. What could he say that would make her want to stay? He let out the breath he'd been holding. "I *feel* like . . . I don't want to let you go."

Meridian smiled; she rose from her position nestled into his body. She dropped a soft kiss on his lips. He lifted his eyes to meet hers; she brushed pieces of hair from his forehead. The affectionate gesture seemed—so strange. "I don't think anyone is asking you to."

"Good."

Through the layers of fatigue that weighted his body and fogged his mind, he thought he heard her say: "I believe I'm beginning to understand."

He started to drift. *Don't go. Stay. For a night. Forever. Just. Don't leave . . .*

CHAPTER 10

"Breathtaking"

IS HOW SHE LOOKED IN THE MOONLIGHT.

A few nights after his reconnaissance mission, Callan invited his newly minted *girlfriend* over to watch the hockey game. She showed up looking comfortable in yoga pants, slippers, and the best version of a Blackhawks jersey he'd ever seen. Low-cut in the front and just tight enough—in all the best places.

Meridian slipped onto the couch beside him; legs curled up beneath her, she leaned her head on his shoulder. His hand assumed a neutral position on her knee.

The horn blared on TV. Face-off. A referee blew his whistle. The center sent the puck hurtling backward to his defenseman. Clack. The crowd cheered, then muted. Announcers' voices faded into the background—like the speakers moved out into the hall.

His girlfriend shifted next to him; her fingers touched his chin, tipping his head to look at her.

Callan blinked to dispel the grayish haze he'd decided

to name *the void*. Because when it crept into his mind and vision, the world disappeared into a nothingness.

Meridian's lips moved and she frowned.

Dammit. He stifled a groan. "I wasn't listening."

"I asked if you were going to order pizza."

"Already done. It'll be here before the end of the first period."

"You were off in outer space a minute ago."

He fixed his eyes on the TV. "I wasn't."

"Just"—she soothed fingers through the hair on the back of his neck—"staring at me, then?" Her breath puffed against his ear.

Thousands of shivers trickled through the muscles of his back. In no particular hurry. "Hmm."

His girlfriend gave him that shy smile—the one with a teasing glint in her eyes. It warmed his chest from the inside out. He bent forward and caught her lips into a kiss. She opened her mouth, allowing him to deepen their connection.

He pressed her back into the couch—his hand slipping into her shirt. He skimmed his hand over her ribcage and ran his thumb over the soft, gauzy fabric of her bra. He could feel the nipple harden when he touched it. She gasped and shifted beneath him. Her eyes slipped closed.

He kissed her cheek and continued to tease the tip of her areola, finally peeling down the cup so he could palm the heated flesh beneath.

"We're not going to make it through three periods"—she nibbled at his ear—"like this." Meridian soothed her tongue along the side of his neck. Her teeth grazed his flesh.

He couldn't stop a low moan from escaping. "Uhhhhn." He opened her bra at the center clasp, and slid his knee between hers. He parted her legs so he could shift closer. "Why not?" He moved his hand to gain a strategic hold at the waistband of her pants.

"You know why," her voice rasped. "Ohhhh, Callan . . ."

"I thought you liked hockey."

"I do. It's basketball I hate."

"Should have turned that on."

"Only if you like hockey more than me."

"Never. Not even the Stanley Cup finals."

She sat up and ripped her shirt over her head. He pulled the bra straps from Meridian's shoulders before laying her down. He settled his weight into her, pressing his arousal against the clothed space between her legs. He dipped his head—their mouths meeting, becoming firmer, more insistent. Electric charges sparked through his skin and rolled the length of his spine.

He slipped fingers into the loose band at her hips, and traced a line against her skin. He broke the kiss to mouth down her neck. Soft, enticing noises escaped her lips. He bit and sucked at the flesh of her chest, and felt her arch off the couch when he mouthed over the peak of her breast.

"Callan!"

Nails dug into the skin between his shoulder blades. He had to steel himself against the hot, electric wave that washed through his system. He lifted his head. "You OK?"

"Yessss," she hissed, her head thrown back over the arm of his couch—her hands pawing at his shirt.

"One of us has to answer the door when pizza arrives."

She groaned. "I hate pizza."

"You don't."

"I hate it right now. I want your shirt off."

"You can wait ten minutes. I've been waiting almost two months."

"If it had been you, shirtless, fixing my car—I might have jumped you then."

"Liar." He kissed her again. He slid his hand into her pants—fingers smoothing over her lace panties. He waited to see if she would twist away.

"Tell me. Tell me something you feel." *Meridian looked at him through lowered lashes.*

"I feel like . . . I don't want to let you go."

The patience of a sniper. He used to hate it. Waiting. Watching. Aching. Breathing. Boring.

At least nothing about waiting for her was dull.

He brushed his hand over her mound, pushing his finger into dampened cloth—in search of her sensitive nub. He found it with the knuckle of his index finger and pressed. His girlfriend whimpered. Hazy blue-green eyes met his. She gasped and panted.

He used his forearm to push her leg back into its position. Callan circled his knuckle into her clitoris again. He grinned as she moved her hips, grinding against his hand. "What do you want?"

"I don't knoooow." Meridian let her head fall back.

She writhed beneath his touch. Her breasts bare, her chest arched. His girlfriend's hips thrust against him. She moaned. "I want you."

Callan took a deep breath and attempted to calm his racing pulse. Rational thought told him he couldn't take her on the couch. He stood from the sofa, bent down, and scooped her up.

He cradled her against his chest, carrying her the short distance to his bedroom. He kicked the door shut, laid her on his bed, and pulled her slippers from her feet. Callan stripped off her yoga pants and panties in one go.

He yanked his shirt over his head, and shed his own pants and boxers.

He kissed her again, long and lingering, as he crawled into the bed beside her. His hands returned to exploring and teasing her softer form. His girlfriend broke their kiss, one hand cupping his cheek. Her aquamarine eyes glittered.

Callan hovered over her, propped up on one arm, his chest skimming hers as his erection lay nestled near her core.

She held his face in both hands. "There's something . . . I want to tell you."

He closed his eyes and bit back a sigh. "If you want to tell me, I'll listen."

"I . . ." She sucked in a breath. "I love you, Callan."

Dammit. He had to change his pace. His plan. He'd wanted to take his time—kissing, tasting every cell of her skin. Driving her mad with desire. Until the flames of *his* need became *theirs*.

But she'd changed the mission in an instant. Her need was something discrete. Different.

Which meant: this was the time. *This* was the crucial moment.

With her confession lingering in the air, Callan moved. He pressed his length into her tight entrance. Meridian's body stretched around him—pulsing, hot. She created an aching pit in his stomach. He buried himself to the hilt, and let out a long, even breath.

Her face in the moonlight. Silver dusted her lashes. It painted her cheeks in brightness and cast shadows on her abdomen. His girlfriend's brow furrowed and her features contorted.

"Why . . ." She pressed her forehead against his. "Why did you stop?"

"I couldn't breathe."

"Oh?"

"Yeah." He pushed a piece of hair out of her face and curled it behind her ear. "You steal my breath away."

"Callan . . ." She kissed him.

The former Marine lifted himself from the circle of her arms. He pulled his erection out to the tip, then plunged back inside. The friction sparked and soothed at the same time. His first few strokes, he kept at a slow pace—watching her. Eyes closed, features slack, her mouth open and mewling. Sparks turned into flames, and he accelerated their rhythm.

He had waited so long . . .

Too long, that primal urge within him roared as he moved in and out of her body. She arched and stretched and fell beneath him. The aching pit in his stomach turned into a sucking vortex. It chilled the heat from his body;

pulled his will, his gentleness, and left him with cold desperation.

"Meridian . . ." He pressed his thumb into her folds. He worked her clitoris as he continued his cadence, penetrating her body with long, smooth strokes. Her sheath tightened—quavering around his cock. He teased her nipple, biting and drawing his tongue over the puckered flesh.

"Uhn, ohhh. Please," she whimpered. He slicked firm circles into her folds. Her arms around his shoulders tightened; she hardened and stilled beneath him. And then she shuddered, her hands grasping, nails biting; Meridian convulsed as she orgasmed. Her body quaked around him, and she breathed his name.

Callan growled. He needed more.

He increased the speed and force of his thrusts. She clung to his neck as her hips surged to meet him—legs wrapped around his waist. He rasped and struggled for air. He wanted to do this for hours, but he was losing the inward battle for control.

He found her mouth again and bit a rough kiss against her lips. The spicy scent of her perfume caught his attention—recognizable, but different. Another time, he wanted to sample her skin and run his tongue all over her body. Find out if she tasted as spicy-sweet as she smelled.

"Mmmm." She bit his earlobe. "I like this."

He groaned as her hot breath turned his blood into liquid fire. He pounded into her, again and again. He rested his forehead on her collarbone. Heated, swirling waters towed and pulled, until his flesh boiled and his body weakened.

He lost the will to fight. To hold on. And he forgot why he would want to. *She feels so good.* He hefted her hips off the mattress, changing the angle of his thrusts. He slammed into her—driving his arousal deep into her slick, wet sex.

Once, twice.

His cock lengthened, pulsed. He fell forward as the roiling water swept his knees. He crashed into her, burying his face into her shoulder. A last thrust and he came inside her with a hoarse cry.

He lay there, spent—her fingers slipping through pieces of his hair. Callan heaved for air, their bodies still connected. Shivering. Shaking.

Moments stole quietly past. Warm air filled his lungs. A controlled breath. His world stilled. The chaos retreated.

He raised his head and found her eyes. A small frown. A smaller smile. She stroked her thumb over his cheek. Meridian closed her eyes and pressed her forehead against his. "Callan."

He seized her mouth into a kiss. Lips soft and no longer burning. She broke away and whispered, "I love you," with a tenderness that felt fragile and real.

He opened his mouth, but his throat closed. Nothing came out. Pain spasmed in his chest—muscle tightening on itself. He sucked in a choking breath and pulled away. *Don't ask me.*

"You won't say it. Will you?"

"You know." He edged to the far side of the bed. Pain subsided into the void. He hated it, the numbness. His hand trembled. He tucked it against his chest so she wouldn't see. "Don't you?"

"Why can't you say it? Or why *won't* you?"

"You always need words. To say words. And I—those aren't easy words." His chest felt like it was caving in.

"They're very easy words." Her tone turned sharp. Pointed. It jabbed him in the stomach and made him bleed. "Three one-syllable words. You've already said more words trying not to say those words." An abrupt exhale. Rustling. The mattress dipped and moved.

Is she leaving? Don't go. Gray hazed into his vision. The void grew wider, and held out its arms. Warm fingers on his shoulder pulled him back.

Her arms held his sheet around her body. Her features pale, her lips trembling. "You know. I've told you how important it is. Maybe it's just words to you, but they're words that matter."

I know. You've told me how much it means to you. I know. And still I'm like this. God, what's wrong with me?

"Why can't you tell me you love me?"

"Because." Mind blank, his tongue tried to form words he didn't recognize. "I can't. I don't want anything to—to take you away." He turned to face her. *Don't ask. Just know.*

Her eyes widened. She lost the sheet she held like a shield and leaned toward him. "Callan."

He gathered her into his embrace. He leaned into her shoulder, and crushed her against him.

Just know.

"*Hunger*"

IS SOMETHING MORE THAN DESIRE.

"Cold pizza or toast?" Callan said, and lifted his head. His stomach groaned. But his hands and other . . . important parts of his body stiffened. He continued stroking a path down Meridian's soft, supple skin.

His morning situation, despite their activities the night before, felt rather dire.

"Hmm?" Meridian rolled his direction. She wrinkled her nose. "Pizza for breakfast?"

"We didn't have dinner."

"Oh." A pause, then: "Oh!" Her hand flew over her mouth. She giggled. "Sorry. I know how you get about food. You must be hungry."

"Starved."

"Then eat."

He grinned and leaned closer. He ran his tongue from the outside of her shoulder to her neck. He bit down.

She gasped. "Why"—she pushed on his shoulders— "why do I suddenly feel like, um, prey?"

"I'm done hunting."

"Ha ha. I just mean . . . you're looking at me like . . ." Her cheeks flushed, and she pulled the sheet over her chest.

"Like what?"

"Like." She wet her lips; the muscle in her neck moved as she swallowed. "We're not going to be eating breakfast for a while."

"False. I need food. And water. Then I can take you to bed for the day."

"The day? A whole day?"

"Mmmm. I can last a while. The benefit of breathing techniques I learned in the military."

"Wh-what—what does that mean?"

"It means: I want to take my time." He moved closer, pressing his arousal into her hip. "I want you to feel good, Meridian." He moved pieces of her hair from her face.

She shifted and pulled herself into a sitting position. "I —I've obviously not been in a relationship like this." His girlfriend hugged her knees to her chest. "But I imagine a playfulness about the physical—uh, about sex. Is healthy."

He sat up and moved beside her.

"But I just want." Her lips quavered. She let out a sharp exhale. "I want to feel like we're committed. Connected. That your feelings—"

"There's no one else, Meridian."

She stared in the direction of her toes. A deep frown creased her forehead. "But I . . . Why—can't you talk to me?"

"I talk to you more than anyone else."

"Callan. Is there . . . You seem to want me or someone, I

don't know who, to believe you hatched into full adult super-soldier Marine guy. No past, no family, no weaknesses. Do you really think anyone who cares about you—that we need you to be indestructible?"

"I didn't claim that this—that I—would be easy."

"Hmm." Her mouth tightened into a thin line.

Seconds crawled into the space between them. His fingers ached to touch her, to maintain their connection. But he wasn't sure he still had her permission.

"Meridian . . ." His insides twisted and jumbled together, pulling muscle fibers in his chest to the point of breaking.

He took a deep breath. The void hedged in.

Callan exhaled and stared through the scope. A shadow crawled across the rocky surface, indicating where the target paced, below.

Objectives had long since become inhuman. Enemies. Numbers, to keep from thinking of the target as a person—with a family. Someone who would miss them.

"Sighting target one thirteen."

Callan shook the memory away.

Meridian stared, her eyes watery and round. "Callan . . ."

He sighed, and the tightness lessened. Callan leaned down and settled his mouth over hers—drawing her into a slow, syrupy kiss. Her hand slid over the surface of his cheek, holding his face. He pressed her close.

"Please. Talk to me."

"About what."

"This. Us. What you said last night. We should talk."

He turned away.

"Is it just the tough-guy Marine thing?"

"No."

"Then why?"

"It's—" His tongue thickened. Fog drifted in front of his eyes; he dug a knuckle into his quad, and the pain helped him focus. "It's difficult. To explain."

"Will you, someday? Will you promise me—you'll try?"

He nodded. She pulled him closer, her lips ghosting against his—light, gentle. So magnetic.

"What did they do to you?"

He pushed her back into the bed.

Callan couldn't remember a time when he'd held anything as soft as her. Meridian's form spread against his. Her hands drew long strokes down his back; her skin feather light, like his favorite cotton shirt—well washed and broken in.

"Mmmm . . ." The muscles of his shoulders shuddered beneath her touch. He skimmed his hand from her hip to her ribcage. He moved her hair and stroked her neck. She watched him through heavy lids, her flesh puckering beneath his fingers. The shush of her breaths hitched, changed, puffed faster.

"Uhhhhn." Her eyes slipped closed as she arched beneath him. The clean, subtle fragrance of her skin; the heady scent of coconut in her hair . . .

Callan kissed her again. The slow connection changed. He stroked her tongue with his; their mouths met, moved, broke apart, and found another way to fit together. Over and over—in what became a fevered pace. He pulled away.

Meridian's eyes peeled open. "Callan." She reached for him. He shed his boxers and moved closer. Her hands grasped his shoulders; she pulled him down for another kiss.

He settled over her again. Bodies crushed together, Callan kissed her—long and deep. He left her mouth to trail his tongue down the side of her neck. Callan cupped her breast, rubbing his thumb in light, teasing circles around its peak. Her breathing changed. Sharp, shallow gasps and feminine mewling—told him what kind of effect he was having on her.

"Mmm, tell me what you like."

"Uhn. I like you," she rasped.

His erection lurched, and wanted to find her heat, again. Callan breathed in, cleared his mind, and focused on Meridian. He continued his exploration.

He bit kisses against the junction of her neck and shoulder. He mouthed over her collarbone to her sternum. Traced his tongue across her flesh. He seized the nipple of her other breast with his lips.

"Uhn, oh, uh! Oooooh."

Callan whispered against the sensitive pebble. He flicked his tongue into the center. Mindless whimpers continued to float into the air. He pressed his length against the junction between her legs.

"Please?"

He stilled. Another—long—inhale. Followed by a measured exhale. He returned to licking and biting the center of her breast; he held her other nipple between his thumb and forefinger, and lightly twisted. Her entire body tightened beneath him, then released. The flat of her foot scraped the length of his calf. Her hips rose off the bed.

"Callan, please?"

He met her gaze; glazed eyes stared back. "Mmm?" He lowered his head and bit at her areola. Meridian hissed. She thrust against him.

"Uhn! Oh, God."

He continued mouthing his way down her chest. He nipped teasing kisses just above her navel before moving lower. Callan pulled one leg over his shoulder. He glanced up. Her eyes clamped shut, her lips parted. Meridian's fingers twisted in his fresh new sheets.

He dipped his tongue into her folds. Meridian squirmed.

"Trust me," he said in a hushed voice.

"It's!" Huff. Pant. "You don't have to. To do that."

"I want to. Relax."

"I—I can't." She thrashed. "I feel like—your touch is fire, and my whole body is melting."

"Good." He scraped his tongue against her nub. Meridian's body jolted. Her hips rocked against him in small, jerky movements.

"Oh, God. Ohhhh."

He licked and sucked at her center. She lifted her palms to her neck and ran them over her chest. The knuckle of her index finger fit between her teeth.

Callan smiled and flicked his tongue in a rapid movement.

"Uhn! Callan! Oh!" Her hands grabbed the pillow behind her head. He laved circles into her folds; her long, lean thighs trembled around him. Callan switched to using his thumb—for a firmer touch. He slicked the digit in fixed, rigid circles against her clitoris.

Meridian's mewling filled the air. Her body rose and fell; tightened and released. The erotic sight lit a fire in his stomach. It burned into his groin.

"Oh, oh, oh!" Meridian arched off the bed and hardened. Silence for just a moment, like she stopped breathing. Tremors turned into quakes. His girlfriend lurched forward, her voice turned raw and desperate: "Oh, God, Callan!"

She crashed back down into the sheets. "Ohhhh."

Callan wasted no time in flipping her over. He lifted her to her knees and pressed his cock into her hot, quivering center. The aftershocks of her orgasm coaxed at his length—urging him deeper inside.

He inhaled and held it as he pulled out of her channel, then delved back inside. She rocked forward beneath him; he exhaled. He paced himself, his thrusts slow, measured. He moved in and out—mouthing kisses against her neck and shoulder. He palmed her breast. The wonder of her skin: soft, silken, heated. He ran his thumb over the sensitive peak.

"Uhnnnn. Callan . . ."

He reeled himself in. He sat back and pulled her into his lap—their bodies still connected. He ran his hands over her chest. His fingers tightening, squeezing. He toyed with her nipples as he continued to rock against her hips.

"Uh. Uh. Uh." Her gasps shushed in time with his thrusts. Her whimpers caused his insides to burn. Flames licked his body and seeped through his pores.

He worked to contain the fire; long, even breaths helped to tamp it down to a well-controlled smolder.

"Meridian . . ." Callan bit her ear. He slid one hand down, over her stomach; her folds already spread, he slicked a finger over that tender little nub again. His girlfriend pitched forward, breaking their rhythm.

"Callan! What? What are you—"

"Shhhh." His left arm clutched her body. He kissed her neck, her shoulder. His right hand continued to work her clitoris. His shaft pulsed in and out of her center.

She squirmed. "But!"

"What's wrong?"

"I just—" She pulled at his hand between her legs; he paused.

"Tell me."

"You—you already . . . I mean—I—" She ducked her head. "I already enjoyed this. I thought it was—y-your turn."

He nipped at her earlobe and let out a low chuckle. "There's no law against you coming a second time."

"What?"

"If you'll let me, I'll do this all day. Or at least a solid hour or two." He drew a light, teasing circle against her clit. He cupped her breast—caressing, fondling its center.

"Uhhhh." She arched and threw one arm over his shoulder. Her hips thrust backward, against his.

"I've waited."

"Yes."

"Been patient."

"Yes." Her pace increased. He let her move; instinct

taking over as she slid, clawed, and bucked. Her sheath tightened.

Trembling. Gasping. Moaning.

"I've been starving. And I'm still—" His control began to slip; he growled. "So hungry."

She clamped down on his erection as an orgasm ripped through her. Meridian doubled over, catching herself on her palms.

Callan shifted gears and rose from his seated position behind her. He planted one leg on the floor for additional leverage; he pumped into her—a few smooth strokes. Embers. Smoking, igniting.

Too much. He grabbed her hips and intensified the force —pounding into her with a burning, raging need. He penetrated her softness. Her rasping breaths turned to loud cries.

It fueled the anguish, burned the last of the air from his lungs.

"Arrrrah!" He came hard, his length bursting deep inside her. Meridian's center quaked around him. She panted. A shiver ran through the muscles of her back.

This. Her. I'll never ask for anything else, I swear.

AFTER A FEW HAZY MOMENTS—OF LOUD BREATHS AND groaning muscles—Callan's arousal slipped from her body. Meridian collapsed onto the mattress and rolled over. She pulled at wet pieces of hair stuck to her cheek.

"We were supposed to eat first."

A different type of fog tugged at his consciousness.

Instead of the emptiness of *the void*, this was a satisfied full-ness—tinged with warmth. He lay beside her, and laced their fingers together.

"We can eat now. Before round three."

"Round three? Will I ever leave your bed again?"

"Do you really want me to answer that?"

She mumbled something that sounded like: "We do have jobs. And other things . . ."

Her chest rose and fell. A sight to behold on its own. "Sure. But not today."

"Not today?" She turned her head and pressed her fore-head against his neck. "All right, but you're cooking."

"Hmm, bad idea."

"So is me being naked and in your clutches, apparently."

"That. Is the best idea we've had."

"Hmmm." Meridian disentangled herself from his loose embrace. "I think I should go."

She rose and scooted toward the end of the mattress.

"Suit yourself. I'll just be here, naked."

Meridian turned and met his gaze. One eyebrow lifted as she swept her eyes down the length of his body. The tip of her tongue touched her lips.

His erection recovered under her gaze.

"Y-you're still . . . hungry?" Her complexion turned a deep crimson.

He sat up and moved toward her side of the bed. "Starved. For real food."

"You said that last time. And you can be such a bear when you don't eat." She stood from his bed. Her naked rear bobbed as she looked for something on the floor. Firm, rounded flesh, and just a glimpse of her—black fabric interrupted the appealing view.

She pivoted; his topless girlfriend cinched the waistband on a pair of his shorts, knotting a double bow in the laces. He gained his feet; he crossed the room, pulling a pair of clean boxers from the top drawer of his dresser. He grabbed a white undershirt from the same tray and handed it to her.

She tugged it over her head. It gapped at the neck, and fell to midthigh. Without a bra underneath, it was the best thing she'd ever worn.

He wanted to tear it off her. With his teeth. "On second thought—"

"Toast and coffee sounds like a plan." She strode from the room.

Cold air swept inside; it chilled the sweat on the back of his neck. He let out a frustrated groan and hurried after her.

He caught her at the edge of his kitchen.

"Oh!" Meridian said as he grabbed her from behind. Callan wrapped his arms around her waist. His hands and lips still thirsted for her skin.

He kissed her behind her ear. Mouthed along her earlobe. His palms scraped over her abdomen—up, toward her ribcage.

"Callan." His girlfriend melted against him. "We're in the kitchen." One arm slipped over his shoulder; her other hand tipped his chin toward her. Meridian's mouth met his, her tongue sweeping between his lips. He maneuvered her around to face him.

"Uhnnnn, Meridian . . ." He moved one hand up, over her breast. The other worked at the knot holding up his shorts.

"What," she hissed, "are you doing?"

"Helping." He walked her backward. The knot obstacle eliminated, the shorts fell to the floor. He kissed her deeply; her arms curled around his shoulders. An instinctual pride flashed through him as he hefted her onto his kitchen table.

"Helping?"

He tugged the T-shirt over her head, then pressed her back—flat against the table. Meridian's breasts mashed against his chest. He spread her legs around his waist, positioning his arousal at her entrance again.

"Meridian," Callan breathed as he entered her body. Her mouth met his—hard, fervent.

He thrust inside her. She wrapped her legs around his waist and moved with him.

"We, uh, ah, ah," she huffed. "M-may starve. If you—ahhhh. K-keep this up. Ah."

"I'm not doing my job, if you can still think." He found the bundle of nerves between her legs—teasing and enticing her body with now-practiced maneuvers.

"Uhn! Callan!" Meridian cried, and whimpered, and purred—as he brought her a third time.

All I'm asking. He sagged over her, his body close to spent.

She ran her fingers through the hair on the back of his neck. Everything about her: soft, warm, accepting. Even as he felt hard, cold, and wrong.

"I love you. And I'll keep telling you that," she whispered. "Until you get it."

Just—don't take her. He kissed her again as the void threatened. It swirled around his kitchen, dulling his senses. *Not her.*

CHAPTER 12

"Unromantic"

MEANT UNMET EXPECTATIONS.

Ten months later

The best and worst thing about Meridian was that Callan always knew where he stood with her. The best —because he'd never been good at *guessing* what women were thinking. And she rarely stayed silent about what she wanted.

The worst because there was no denying when she was pissed. Especially at him.

Abrupt responses to his text messages. Refusing to pick up the phone when he called. Callan had learned to give her space. And to steel himself to be present when she was ready to talk.

Tuesday morning, he arrived at the gym, before her, and headed to the treadmill to begin his HIIT training. He set up his workout program and hit "start." He began with a brief two-minute warmup.

Deep breaths, the rhythmic beat of his footfalls. The

steady flash of the heart monitor. Routines were simple. Sometimes the lack of focus could be soothing.

Other times . . .

Callan doubled over and huffed. Waves of agony crashed through him. "I—I can't, Sergeant. I'm done. Arm's busted. Ankle's sprained."

"You think the enemy gives a GODDAMN that you hurt? They'll put you out of your misery. Or worse, you'll get your squad killed. Are you the weakest link?"

He flinched but straightened. He pushed against the haze. "No, sir."

"Tell me, soldier: ARE YOU THE WEAKEST LINK?"

Callan wheezed. The heart monitor beeped—alerting him he'd reached one hundred percent of his target heart rate.

He backed the speed down on his treadmill to recover. It notified him that he was a solid seven minutes into his workout. He sucked in air and glanced at the machine beside him. *Shit. Where is she?*

Ten minutes into his HIIT session, Meridian arrived. Callan took measured strides as he recovered from sprinting. He met her gaze for a second. She shot him a glare.

Not a good start.

He took a deep breath and watched her stab her treadmill dashboard—setting her speed a good half mile per hour faster than her usual pace. Her long ponytail swayed as she began to walk. Dark-pink shoes trod heavily against the running deck.

Callan sighed. His heart-rate monitor showed that his pulse was back in the green zone. *Time to sprint.* He increased his speed and moved from a slow jog into a thirty-second all-out run. His body thrummed and his lungs burned. His heart raced with the effort.

By the time he moved into the one-minute recovery, his girlfriend's cheeks puffed with every breath. Her skin glistened a darker shade of pink; sweat slicked the hair around her ears. She edged back her speed.

"Good morning," he puffed out.

"Is it?" she huffed in reply.

"Thought so?"

"I didn't."

He blew out a breath. "What'd I do this time?"

"You know damned well"—gasp, pant—"what you did!"

"I thought you'd like it?" Callan wheezed. He looked down at the time. *Shit. I need to sprint.* He pressed the button to increase his speed.

Meridian reached over and clicked the "4" button to return him to a fast walk. "You thought I'd *like* it?"

"You've had clothes and a toothbrush at my place for months. You even brought over your latest foster dog last week."

That earned him a pointed glare.

"And your lease is almost up."

"So you ask me to move in with you! You don't leave me an 'add a lessee' form under my door—with those little arrow stickers that say 'sign here.'"

He shrugged. "Seemed easier."

She growled at him and yanked the red cord on his treadmill. It lurched to an emergency stop. He caught himself on the rails to keep from face-planting into the control panel.

"Meridian."

She pushed her stop button, then stepped down from her machine.

He leapt to the floor and grabbed her arm. "I don't get it."

"Of course you don't!" She wrenched from his grip. His girlfriend glanced around the gym before hissing in a half whisper, half yell, "You're the most"—her fists shook in midair—"infernal, aggravating, not to mention stubborn—"

"You just did."

"—unromantic jerk I've ever met!" She stamped a foot against the rubber flooring. It made a mild, hollow sound.

"But you do want to move in with me."

"That's not the point! You're supposed to ask. With flowers and—"

"Pretty words?"

She drew herself up and squared her shoulders. "Yes. Sometimes I want pretty words, Callan. Not all the time. But sometimes. The important times." His girlfriend crossed her arms. Her eyes sparked, and sweat slicked pieces of hair against her cheek. "Moving in together is supposed to be a *next step* in a long-term, more serious commitment. There should be pretty words for that." Her mouth formed a tight line, and her eyebrows pinched into a frown.

"What do you want me to say? Please move in with me?"

"I want a date where you dress up and wear something other than the one blazer you seem to own."

He stared at a point over her shoulder. The void drifted in.

"You know what? We're done. Don't call me. Just put my things in the hallway. I'm done with whatever this is, Callan."

She whipped around and stormed off. Out the fitness-center door . . .

Fuck!

THE PROBLEM WITH BUYING AN ANGRY GIRLFRIEND flowers was never so apparent as when said girlfriend lived across the hall. The red rose petals could have served a better purpose than filling trash bags on his doorstep. *Especially for the cost.* Callan sighed.

A faint bark sounded from the other side of her door. The little beagle pup Meridian had agreed to foster—the cleverest dog in the rescue shelter, in Callan's opinion. The little guy had sniffed out the best situation a pet could want.

"He's a sweet boy. He just needs a name. And a home." *The sand-colored puppy curled up in the crook of her arm. Eyes shut tight, he looked like he was sleeping as hard as he could.*

His princess, he'd found out, had a long history of volunteer work at animal rescues and pet-adoption centers. Still, she was more likely to leave food and water in bowls behind the apartment complex than to take on more than was reasonable for fostering. It helped that their complex only allowed one pet per apartment.

He knew how attached she'd become to the small dog, but she was a pragmatic princess. And had been steeling herself for weeks to give the pup away—as soon as someone agreed to adopt him.

Callan sighed and crossed his arms. The fluffy thing took up space in Meridian's lap, dragged them out of bed too early on weekends. And had interrupted their other bedroom activities a time or two.

He took a last look at the colorful mess littering the hall. *I should leave well enough alone, shouldn't I?*

"PTSD is very treatable." A white-coated windbag prac- *tically recited paragraphs from the little medical brochure they handed out at the VA. "We're making new discoveries every year. People just like you can fully—"*

"Doesn't matter."

He closed the door to his apartment with his back and leaned against the metal. His recent physical had turned out just like all the others. Bunch of doctors who thought he needed some disability diagnosis. *I don't need their brochures or therapy bullshit. Most days I don't feel anything. Which is only a problem when I'm with her.*

Her livid features had been burned into his irises.

"Moving in together is supposed to be a next step in a long-term, more serious commitment. There should be pretty words for that."

He grumbled at himself. *You know why she's like this. That shithead boyfriend ghosted her. And then there was her father, who never said anything he should have.*

It's just some words, Brand. Why can't *you do that for her?* He glanced at his phone. *Well, one reason, currently, is that she's avoiding me. So, I'll need a plan.*

CALLAN FOUND THE REFRIGERATOR MAGNET WITH THE name of Meridian's favorite animal rescue. He found their website on his phone and submitted an interest form for the beagle. *I'm betting my future with* her *on a four-legged furball. But this affords me several opportunities.*

His phone lit with the caller: Unlisted. *Maybe that's the shelter?*

"This is Brand," he said as he answered the phone.

"Aha! I knew the princess type would teach ya some manners. You even know how to answer your phone now." Watts's voice boomed through the speaker.

Callan not-so-inwardly groaned. "Why are you on my phone, asshole?"

"Whoa. You know, you could do a whole side-hustle thing with like that super grumpy shit-my-dad-says kinda greeting cards."

"Who the hell buys greeting cards anymore?"

"Not an expert, but I think the main buyers these days are boyfriends." A light chuckle. "You know, the kind who happen to be in the doghouse with their girlfriend. Possibly ex-girlfriend."

I walked into that one. "That's why you're on my phone."

"Dude, look. I haven't gotten in your face about this because you were gonna handle it."

Callan held the thing away and snarled at the handset. The mouth on the other end kept chattering. ". . . time to listen to the doctors. Stop being a stubborn ass—"

"This isn't your fuckin' business."

"*You are* my fuckin' business. And I don't want this to go sideways for you. Never mind the fact that she's nice, and beautiful. She clearly has a healthy dose of savior complex that reminds me of a certain someone."

How long do I have to listen to this? He set the phone on the counter and turned away.

"I'll help you, this time. And then you need to get some help, therapy, something. Deal?"

Callan stared at the device. "No. I don't need your help. I'm not playing some high-school telephone game with you, your girlfriend, and Meridian. I'm hanging up. Fuck off."

"Yeah, fuck you—"

Callan clicked the button to end the call. *Asshole. I don't need his interference. I play the hero, adopting her "Baby," who's gonna get a new name. Raider's good. And I'll get her to talk to me at the very least. And then flowers and dinner and . . .*

I will need to get this right on the first try. Or I'm going to be out of my apartment. And starting a petting zoo as a "side hustle."

STEP ONE IN A HOSTILE NEGOTIATION: FIND NEUTRAL ground. Callan adjusted his collar and eyed the glass door to the Cap'n Ruffs animal rescue.

Step two: offer something the other party wants in an attempt to defuse the hostility. In his pocket were two printed tickets, representing a weekend getaway that he'd arranged. A phone call to his friend and former employer Rayan Wali had provided a destination and transportation.

Rayan had offered up his time-share condo in the Florida Keys and chartered company jet—all within a very short phone call.

A home for Raider, the pretty words she wants, and a weekend away. If this doesn't do it, I'm sunk.

Callan opened the door. A lady greeted him, then escorted him to the back. Meridian sat in the corner of the large play area, cradling Baby. The rescue worker let him in through the gate.

She glanced up. Her eyes grew wide, and she stood. "What are you doing here?"

"Adopting our dog."

"Come again?"

"I'm sorry, Meridian." He dropped to one knee and took her hand; he pressed it to his lips.

Crimson lines streaked her neck. Her features flushed and she glanced around. "What are you doing? Get up. Dogs pee on this floor."

He grimaced, but pressed on. He handed her a jewelry gift box from the pocket of his blazer. She eyed him, but lifted the top. Inside was Raider's collar, with a little bow-tie decoration, and both their names and phone numbers engraved. "I hope the number's still the right one. I haven't been able to verify it still works."

"You're the one adopting Baby?"

"Raider. I think it suits him."

"Of course you'd name your dog Raider."

"Our dog. I'm still hoping you'll do me the honor of moving in with me."

She patted the puppy's fuzzy head. "New blazer."

"Even had it tailored."

"I suppose there are more flowers and some reservations at a nearby restaurant." A little tug at the corner of her mouth. A suspicious glance.

"That's where you're wrong."

"Oh?" She straightened her shoulders and met his gaze.

Callan handed her the ticket printouts.

"Good for one luxurious weekend getaway with your hot live-in boyfriend. And an asterisk with a note at the bottom: not a stalker." She laughed. "I'm pretty sure you're insane. And seriously, get up off the floor. You'll want to wash those when you get home."

"Spent longer in worse places."

"Callan? This was sweet. And over the top, but I suppose I did shut you out. And didn't give you much choice."

"I always have a choice. So do you. You're important to me, and I should do better." Hot dread sank into his abdomen. "Even if I'll never deserve you." Callan rose to his feet. *I want this. I want you.* He pulled her into his arms.

"You're the only one I want to be with. And I try to

understand . . . But sometimes you're just—" She took a breath. "So closed."

He didn't know what to say. But he didn't doubt it was true. That heated ache burrowed further into his stomach. "We'll need to pack for the weekend."

"A vacation together?" She snuggled into his chest. "You do know how to win me over, don't you?"

God, I hope so. I don't think I'd survive long without you. Not anymore. He ducked his head and gave her a quick kiss.

"Oh, what about Baby—er, Raider?"

"Watts already offered to dogsit while we're gone." He snapped the sleepy beagle's collar around his neck. The fuzzball opened his eyes and yawned.

"I wonder if he knows Nora's allergic to dogs."

Callan tamped down his desire to laugh. He could just picture his *buddy's* face, and how easy it would be to guilt-trip the guy despite Nora's probable aversion. *He's about to find out.*

"I was thinking they probably need a nice cat."

He sighed. "You can't save them all, you know."

"Mmmm, yeah, I know. But I'll keep trying."

CHAPTER 13
Numb"

NOT THE SAME AS EMPTY.

Spur-of-the-moment missions, without the usual analysis and obsessive details—the possibility of failure rose by a significant factor. But sometimes, the potential reward greatly outweighed the increased risk factor.

Like today.

In this particular case, a last-minute getaway weekend had the potential to pay off by soothing any lingering doubts or ruffled feathers Meridian might have about *officially* moving in together. And it could give them uninterrupted time—something that, with their respective work schedules, had been a little more difficult of late.

Part of why he'd asked her to move in . . .

THEY ARRIVED AT A VERY MILITARY-STYLE AIRPLANE hangar—except it looked pristine. "Military grade" was a gross misnomer. Soldiers often complained about supplies from the lowest-cost bidder—with good reason.

Hangars were some of the worst examples. No need for the installations to be painted or look pretty. They had to blend in with their surroundings, so rust and debris were common decorations.

But Rayan's operation was backed by ample funding. And made a solid profit. Plenty of corporate clients paid good money to provide security to executives traveling to unstable nations of the world. His employees, often referred to as "Mercs" behind closed doors, had top-of-the-line gear, received top-of-the-line pay. It was a great gig. Until it wasn't.

"You sure you're all right?" The young CEO frowned. He scratched at his beard and focused his full attention on Callan.

"I'm fine." The line fell easily from Callan's lips. "It's just the lack of sleep."

Stern hazel eyes met his gaze from across the room. The second-generation American still held fast to his Jordan heritage and customs. It was a unique mix to hear him speak with a Midwestern accent while wearing a more traditional-style linen shirt, chinos, and loafers.

"It's not getting better, my friend. You have this look about you. Worn, weary." Rayan pulled closed lips into a thin smile. The man was always complaining about appearances. He bemoaned his own baby-faced features, saying women always wanted a bad boy. And he grumbled when his team didn't have their uniforms pressed to perfection.

"Will it help to take some time off? I know a guy. Some

*baby-faced asshole who happens to like you." His mouth split
into a wide grin.*

*Callan shifted from one foot to the other. He stared at the
floor. "I think it's best if I resign."*

*"You could take a leave of absence instead, you know."
Rayan's hand gripped his shoulder. "You're always welcome
here."*

Rayan had hated for him to go, but the job had two
major problems: First, it made Callan's "healthy dose of
paranoia" tip out of the realm of healthy and into *obsessive*
territory. Always on alert. Wired. Sleepless.

And second, the lack of a stable home life lost its appeal.
He'd saved up some money, but didn't even have a place to
store a car or furniture. Living out of suitcases and hotels
was worse than the military. He found himself asking the
question: "What's the point in living at all?" one night. And
decided it was time to do something different.

And here he was. *This is definitely different.*

Callan rubbed his palm over his left wrist. He flexed
and relaxed his hand. But the tremors shook his fingers.

Rayan was easy to spot; his well-kept mop of silvery-
white hair, long blue jacket, and wide grin provided a sharp
contrast to the dark-suited, close-cropped, serious-natured
members of his security team for hire.

"Callan Brand, it's good to see you, my friend."

Callan shook the guy's hand and gave him a polite nod.

"Same old Brand. Although it seems, well, she's new."
He tilted his head, glancing over Callan's shoulder. "I hope
you'll enjoy the, ah, accommodations." His already wide
grin grew wider.

187

"Appreciate the favor."

"Oh, it was no trouble! I was glad you called. And happy to repay you for some of the cyber stuff. What my lawyers refer to as events, and I'll stop there before I get in trouble. But I've appreciated your help over the past couple of years."

Callan nodded.

"Have you two been together long?"

"Almost a year."

"That's wonderful." He beamed. "I can't wait to meet her."

Callan managed to rein in the urge to rub a hand over his face. The man could walk a few feet and say hello. Instead, the CEO stuffed his hands in his pockets and rocked back on his heels. He cast an exaggerated glance at Meridian, then back at the former Marine.

Callan set his jaw.

"You'd make me ask you? Fine, fine. My friend, will you *please* introduce me to your beloved?"

Callan groaned. *Beloved?*

"Or is there some reason you're keeping her to yourself?"

"You can meet her," Callan said with a sigh, and shook his head. Rayan slapped him on the back as they fell into step. The two men made their way toward Meridian.

"She reminds me of someone. And you know how good I am at remembering faces . . ."

This is why I would have flunked out of Prince Charming school.

A FAMILIAR FIGURE STEPPED FORWARD AND HELD OUT A set of parachute packs. The man stood a couple of inches taller than Callan. Wearing a standard-issue flight suit, the only thing out of place was the airman's dagger, tucked into a leg holster.

"Nolan."

The former Air Force pilot was shockingly lethal—if you were on the wrong side of his code of loyalty. Which was, in Callan's opinion, a bit too complex.

"You'll need these." Renzo "Ren" Nolan frowned as he delivered the lame, overused tactic. Meridian wrapped her arms around the pack.

"Good luck." He turned and took measured steps in the opposite direction.

The asshole pulled off a perfect performance. Rookies bought it every time. Nolan possessed the uncanny ability to pinch his face into a serious expression faster than Callan's first drill sergeant. It helped sell the joke.

Meridian gasped; wide, panicked eyes sought his. "Please tell me we're not—"

"We're not. Nolan just has a bad sense of humor."

"Nolan?"

"Renzo Nolan. Our pilot. It's a normal flight. With a normal landing."

"I wonder about this group's definition of normal." She arched an eyebrow. "Including yours."

Callan shoved his hands in his pockets and walked to the front of the aircraft. "Not funny, flyboy."

"It was a little funny. The look on her face was worth it."

Callan crossed his arms. "Guess you drew short straw?"

"Rayan asked me to do it," he said with a shrug. "That one seems a little prissy. Not like you ever had a type. But that . . ." He gestured in Meridian's direction. Three pieces of matching pink luggage sat at her feet. She wore high heels and a miniskirt.

I'm not complaining.

"Not what I would have guessed."

"Hmm. She looks the part. But she's got a healthy dose of tenacity mixed with her sugar and spice."

"And everything nice?" A slow smile spread over the man's features. Nolan's head tipped to the side as he continued to stare.

The hair on the back of Callan's neck stood on end. His heart thumped against his ribcage. "She's not your type."

"Long-legged blondes are my kryptonite. And hers are a mile long." Nolan glanced away. He took two steps up the airstair and leaned into the cockpit. The pilot flipped a few overhead switches, then glanced back over his shoulder. "Apparently she's worth every bit of the drama, too, if you're fucking her."

"Not much drama. Just . . ." Callan said, and shrugged. "Too much pink."

"Come now." Nolan skipped down from the airstair. The smug grin on his face made Callan want to hurl, or punch his former colleague in the gut. Or both. "I'm sure her pink things are some of her best features."

Callan growled; he shoved Nolan, forcing the guy back,

against the aircraft. The pilot's hand found his dagger. He clutched the knife, blade down near his collarbone.

Callan lifted his hands. Nolan blinked; he shook his head. "Sorry. Habit." Thin, colorless lips pressed together.

It wasn't a smart move—picking a fight with him. Nolan had mastered several martial-arts forms over the years. His favorite was kali, a defensive weapons-based fighting style. The last time the two of them had knuckled up, there had been no clear winner.

Just several hours in the emergency room—complete with Rayan pacing the floor and praying a dua over them.

"The only pink things you can think about are her suitcases."

Nolan snorted and rolled his eyes.

"Unless you want to be ejected midflight without a chute. I'm sure I can remember how to land."

The flyboy gripped Callan's shoulder as he all but doubled over with laughter.

"What's funny?"

Nolan straightened, but couldn't or wouldn't hide his face-splitting grin. "You. It seems she's had some effect on you."

"Just don't tell me to write greeting cards as a side hustle."

Nolan laughed harder.

THE SIZE AND LUXURIOUS QUALITY OF RAYAN'S timeshare shouldn't have surprised Callan. But if he'd had an entire bunker to himself, it still would have seemed smaller. And definitely nowhere near as fancy. He'd stayed in some opulent hotels during his time with Wali Private Security, but his job was to be on alert.

Hyperaware of every movement. The level of focus required approached exhausting. But not this time. *I can't remember the last time I took a vacation.*

Wooden floors gave way to polished marble—with glittery flecks. Walls held every sort of decoration he could have imagined, and then some: canvas, hand-painted tiles; a mural adorned one panel of the bedroom's interior wall. Glass doors gave way to a large balcony, complete with ornate iron railing.

"This place is amazing. You and Rayan must be close friends."

"Why do you say that?"

"Well, he did fly you and your plus-one to the coast, and then loaned you his condo—just because you asked him to?"

"He owes me a few favors."

"Some favors." Meridian wrapped her arms around him. His duffel still dangled from two fingers over his shoulder.

"Did I hear Nolan correctly? The complex has its own private beach?"

"Yeah. Rayan owns one of the cabanas."

"That sounds amazing!" She grinned up at him with sparkling blue-green eyes. "You really went all out, Callan."

"I didn't mean to . . ." He gently untangled himself from her embrace—long enough to throw his duffel bag aside. "To take you or our relationship for granted, Meridian." He pulled her into his chest.

She fiddled with the chain around his neck. "Thank you. I think we've both been taking each other a little for granted. We need to make an effort, both of us, to protect our time—to just, ah, enjoy. Being with the other person."

"I thought if you moved in, that would be easier. But now we have a puppy."

"Yeah. But he's adorable. And so worth it. You'll see."

I hope he's chewing his way through Watts's place. Callan swallowed a smile. "So, what do you want to do first?"

"Mmmm. So many choices. Beach or hot tub. Local eateries? Guaranteed to have fresh seafood."

"I did rain-check you dinner."

"But." Her voice hit a sultry note, filled with promise. Certain parts of his body noticed.

"But?"

"How long has it been?"

A cold sweat formed on the back of his neck. "Since?"

Meridian ran her hands over the front of his T-shirt. She cupped his face and drew him into a long, slow kiss. Her mouth, well practiced at melding to his—stoked the burning embers inside. Her flame flickered. He pulled her closer.

She broke away. "Since this."

"Too long." He brought his mouth down over hers. Lips thinned as their kisses turned harder, desperate. His fingers skimmed over her waist, slipping up to undo her bra.

Meridian gasped. "Bed—bedroom."

193

He groaned. His girlfriend took his hand and tugged him down the hall—to the master bedroom. He sat on the bed as she shut the door.

She turned and wasted no time joining him on the mattress. Callan kicked off his shoes and pulled his shirt over his head. Meridian discarded her blouse; her bra dipped and came loose. She let it drop to the floor.

Her breasts instantly commanded his full attention.

Meridian's full, beautiful chest bounced and rippled and swayed as she wriggled out of her miniskirt. Callan stood. He yanked his belt, undid the button on his jeans, and pushed them to the floor.

His panty-clad girlfriend raised an eyebrow as she pressed into his arms. She smoothed her hands over his shoulders; her mouth slanted over his. Her tongue swept into his mouth.

He folded his arms around her, drawing her closer. He pulled her with him onto the bed.

Callan palmed her breast as he nudged her onto her back. He settled his weight against her; his length pressed against the panty-covered junction between her legs. She seethed.

"Is this what you wanted?" He nipped kisses down her neck. Her arms tightened around his shoulders; fingernails bit into his skin.

"I miss," Meridian sighed, "feeling connected to you." He drew a line with his tongue over her collarbone and down; he circled the peak of her breast. She moved her hips against him. "You pull away from me, sometimes. But this —" She gasped as he laved the center of her nipple. His fingers found the other bud; he traced the edge of it, and lightly squeezed.

"When we're together—uhn!—like this." One foot ran over his calf—to lock behind his knee. She thrust against him.

His entire body panged. He paused, raised his head to look at her. Meridian's other leg wrapped around his waist.

Dazed eyes met his. Blue fire burned within. "I feel like —you're here. With me."

She pulled him into another kiss; Callan went willingly. Syrupy-soft and pliable, her lips caressed his. Her fingers soothed and tangled in his hair.

He broke the kiss and sat up. He shucked his boxers. "I'm always here with you."

"You're not. And I miss you when you go . . .wherever it is you go."

He tugged her panties from her hips and discarded them. He settled over her again.

"I know your job can be difficult; secretive. But I get the impression"—a lopsided smile—"you're not thinking about your work."

"Definitely not now. You. Stop thinking of all that."

One eyebrow rose. "Mmmm, make me."

"Your off switch is around here somewhere. Is it here?" He bit and laved at the peak of her breast.

"No. I still want to know"—a loud breath—"how did you know those people? It seemed like you were very familiar with them, what they do. How . . ."

"I spent a year. Working for Rayan." He dipped his head and lapped at her other nipple. "Is this it?"

"Uhn. Still not . . ."

"Where could it be?"

"I thought you were supposed to be good at reconnaissance. You had a whole mission and—"

Callan pressed a finger into her center; he drew a firm circle against her clit.

Meridian hissed, her feet singing over the sheets. Her back arched off the mattress.

"Must have found it." Callan moved up the length of her body, lying beside her on the bed. He continued to work the tender nub between her legs. Her hands gripped the edge of the pillow behind her head; her lips parted. Panting. Moaning. Pleading.

He dipped his head to cover her mouth with his. His princess kissed him back with a hunger, a fervor he recognized; he coaxed her tongue with his.

"Uhn!" She broke the kiss as Callan worked her clitoris —his digit slicking tight, wet patterns into her sex. Meridian's hips grinded against his hand. "Please," her voice rasped. She moaned again.

"Please what?"

"Be here with me. I want you, Callan . . ."

He wasted no time in moving over her, his length finding, sinking into her. That incredible, hazy, softness—so full and so different than the void—it saturated his skin with her heat.

Callan set a slow, measured pace in and out of her body. He held his breath, focused. Her distant cries of pleasure grew closer with every thrust. Her lips against his ear.

Shivers and shudders melted together; she stoked the

fire that burned constantly in her presence—until the burning thrill overtook him.

Too soon. He grumbled; the aftershocks of his climax echoed through his system. The edges of his consciousness began to fade. He gritted his teeth and pushed at the haze.

The shush of her heated breaths; his name whispered against his skin. Her fingers in his hair.

"Ah, Callan."

These moments, like so many embers—disjointed, glowing. They burned away parts of the darkness, flared light where there had only been pain.

And when she became part of him . . .

He could remember, in measured doses, how to feel.

"I love you, Callan."

CHAPTER 14

"Regret"

DISTORTS AND CORRUPTS MEMORIES.

Callan stood on the condo balcony overlooking the ocean. Salted air swirled with a strong breeze; it lifted the hair from his forehead and cooled the sweat along the back of his neck. The crash and splash of waves sounded so near, at first. But the void . . .

He clutched the balcony rail as another spasm rolled through his spine.

"Mission, there's a child." *Callan tried to keep his voice neutral, tried to keep his breathing in check.* They'll call it off. There's too much risk. *He kept his sight trained on the target.*

"Mission objective confirmed."

"There's a child," *he repeated.* Breathe. Natural point of aim. Refocus. Breathe. *His heart pounded. Lungs burned.* Scope shadow. Trigger control. BREATHE, GODDAMMIT!

"Confirm target."

His spotter hissed: "Take the shot!"

He hated that memory. If there was anything he could cut out of his brain and burn to ash, it would be that memory.

Water reflected the light of the full moon. Yellowy-white, the ocean foamed with a little girl's blood.

I let myself get distracted and fell into this trap again. Stop. Don't think. Don't remember. I need to breathe. Nothing good happens . . . when I lose my breath. He doubled over again. A mix of acidic heat and ice swirled and broke against his spine—like how waves slammed against the shore.

"It's not," he gasped, "getting better." Some days, he could swear the whole thing had worsened. "Meridian . . ."

She made him stronger and weaker at the same time.

I need her. Callan wasn't sure how or when it had happened, but he fought the void every day to keep her near. Even still, when he was with her, the nightmares had a habit of coming to the surface.

Trying to escape.

Wind whipped through him. Cold air thrashed at his goggles, his fatigues, his pack; it ripped down his back. A dark terror seared through every nerve ending.

He could manage the visions, and the memories. But the tremors bothered him. And still, nothing ate him from the inside out like the rage . . .

"If you're just going to sit there and ignore me . . ." A red-faced version of Meridian pushed against his shoulder. "I wonder why I bother!"

"What?" Callan glanced up at the sound of her heels

clicking across the floor. She grabbed her purse from the counter. "What's wrong?"

"I've been talking to you for ten minutes. I don't know where you go, Callan. But you're clearly not here"—she turned her head to glare over her shoulder—"with me."

The room tilted at an odd angle. She hadn't been talking to him, had she? He frowned and stood from his sofa. "I didn't realize you needed so much attention, your highness."

"You're such a jerk." She stormed out of his apartment.

Black fog rumbled in, tinged with red. He closed his eyes, tried to clear it all away. His heart raced, drumming an erratic beat. Callan sucked in air, held it, counted. He repeated the effort.

And again.

When his vision finally cleared . . .

His hand throbbed and ached; blood trickled down his leg. The remote control broken—black plastic cutting into his palm. The coffee table upended; the dish that had been resting on its surface lay shattered on the floor.

He hung his head.

I have to find a way to beat this. He leaned over the rail. It's the past. All in the past . . .

He took another deep, cleansing breath. Stared out at the night sky. Listened to the roar of the waves. He let it out.

This only happens—I only can't control it—when I can't find my breath.

Another intake of air. The fear quieted and slunk back into the night.

But it took everything else with it.

"Unlovable"—A word that's just as it sounds.

THEY'D MADE PLANS THE FOLLOWING WEEKEND: THE plan for her move, a plan to tackle the late-year holidays. The couple moved her day-to-day stuff over during the week. And collected their pet from an appropriately frazzled-looking Watts.

The naked version of his girlfriend uncoiled herself and stretched. Her sense of modesty around him had settled in a much better place these days. Her smooth skin rippled; she rolled toward him and gave him a soft smile.

"We don't have to work out today." Her breasts jiggled as she reached for him. "Come back to bed."

He stared at her chest; his "morning situation" remained upright. "Those two statements conflict."

"Oh?"

"If I 'come back to bed,' I intend to work out."

"You! Ugh, terrible." She pulled the sheet over most of her body. One hip, and its long tanned leg, flowed over the fabric.

Callan stripped the cover from her grasp and settled beside her. Meridian squeaked. Then she snuggled against him. He sighed. He knew she needed this, his closeness. But a certain part of his anatomy wasn't satisfied—

". . . again?" Her voice cut into the haze.

"Hmm?"

Fingers, no longer tentative, slid over his clothed erection. He glanced at her out of the corner of his eye.

She grinned. His heart flipped, then flopped. Callan moved, pinning her beneath him on the bed. He hovered over her as she wound her legs and arms around him. Then he lowered his lips to hers.

"Yes, again."

His girlfriend kissed him—pulling him into her softness, holding him close. And he entangled himself with her. Buried his length inside her.

And finally let go.

Her move took the entire weekend. They'd found room for a few pieces of Meridian's furniture—anything she considered *better* than what Callan possessed. Watts showed up to help move heavier things into storage.

It was a process. One that took longer than he'd have liked, but he gave her the space to do things in the way and order she needed. His girlfriend was just different than he was—light and beautiful, with easy smiles. She possessed genuine and warm expressions, like she could give her whole heart away with a look. A significant contrast to the ones Watts wore to hide his pain.

Or even the ones Callan saw in the mirror.

They were so busy moving and working, Thanksgiving sneaked up on them without so much as a warning. Callan and Meridian accepted a last-minute invite from Watts and Nora—to eat too much and watch football.

Callan promised Meridian that they could decide on Christmas plans over the long weekend.

"Oh, um, sure. That sounds . . . nice." Her voice hesitated; she took a deep breath and swallowed.

"You OK?" He moved pieces of hair from her cheek.

A faint curve of her lips. "Ah, yeah, just tired from all the moving. But it's finally done. I just have the cleaning appointment on Tuesday and I can turn in my keys." She pecked his lips.

"Yeah."

Her eyes glimmered. "Are you happy, Callan?"

At first, Callan thought it was the exhaustion from moving. But when she said she didn't even "feel up to" making plans for Christmas, Callan started to wonder what else was going on.

The soft pad of her footsteps along with the excited clip of her four-legged shadow alerted him to Meridian's presence. He glanced up from his report. She stood at the end of the sofa; shoulders sagging, she rubbed a hand over her forehead. An electric hum shushed in the air whenever she was near.

"Are you all right?"

"I'm fine. Just . . ." She eased onto the couch beside him. The faint scent of cinnamon and citrus wafted closer. He closed the cover on his tablet. "Just been a little tired lately."

"I noticed." He studied her profile. Raider pawed at the foot of the couch. He helped the fuzzball into his favorite lap. "Couldn't rouse you to work out."

"Sorry." She met his gaze and stretched her lips, but it

fell miles short of a smile. Meridian rested her head on the plush couch cushion and patted Raider's head. "Maybe I'm coming down with something."

A hot pool of acid began to form in his stomach. He looked away, and focused on the corner of the coffee table. He traced the edge with his eyes. "Is that all it is?"

"I mean, I hope I'm not sick, but—"

"If you're angry . . ." He took a deep breath; the pit in his stomach widened. "We should talk about it."

"I'm not?" She slipped her hand into his and leaned closer. "Callan, I'm not angry with you."

Another breath; air moved into his lungs this time. "So there's nothing wrong?" Her cheeks were pale, and her eyes hazy. "Between us?"

"I mean . . . I always think we could communicate better."

"What do you mean?"

"You really want to deny that?" she said with a sigh and stood up.

"No? But." He reached for her hand. Meridian gave it to him and gasped as he pulled her into his lap. Bleary eyes met his; she gave him a soft kiss. "I hear that's a common issue?"

A slight nod. "It is."

"So."

"So?"

"What should we talk about?" He held her closer. Her warm breath pulsed in time with the blood coursing through his arteries. The feel of her curves; the way she fit against him . . . *Mmmm, she seems softer.*

"Hmm?"

"What's next?"

She lifted her head. "Meaning?"

"Well, as you put it: moving in together is supposed to be a next step." He met her eyes. Wanted her to know and see—he was serious. "What's next? After this."

"This"—she frowned—"isn't enough?"

"For now. But it's not all I want, Meridian."

Her face crumpled, and for a terrible moment, she looked like she might cry. "I told you, I'm not ready." She pulled from his embrace. Found her feet. Moved away.

Heat drained from his body and left him with an icy, bone-deep chill. "You said you weren't sure." Callan stood on numb legs and followed her. "That was a year ago."

"I guess. It's just—" One arm curled over her chest. "That hasn't changed."

"No. Now you seem to *know* you're not ready."

"What do you want, Callan? For me to get out a crystal ball and tell you when our relationship will change? When I will, or you will? People don't work like that."

"Why does something need to change?"

"Because the way things are? I'm not . . ." She pressed her lips together and looked away.

"You're not what?"

"I'm not convinced."

The air in the place froze to a certain stillness. A quiet. Like he was out in the open, and couldn't gauge the enemy's position—or angle of attack. Just that . . . he was exposed. "Convinced of what, Meridian?"

"That you love me." Those blue-green eyes changed.

206

Softened. Ached. "That deep down you love me so deeply, and so much, that . . ." Meridian lowered her head.

"That what?"

"That we could make it for a lifetime. I don't know. I keep waiting for—"

"I have tried. To understand, to accept things at your pace—not mine. I don't know what else I can do. Or say. Dammit, Meridian, I'd lay down my life for you."

"But I don't want that. I don't want you to *die* for me. I'm not a cause. I just want—"

"You just want what?"

"I—I can't explain it. I just—" She hugged her arms over her chest. "You don't—I don't know how to say what I mean, but there's still so much I don't know about you. That you won't tell me!"

"Like what?" He took a steadying breath. The hot liquid in the pit of his stomach continued to rise.

"Like *things.*"

"What. Things. What have I failed to explain. That you've asked—"

"You never say how you feel! About me, about anything! Your entire vocabulary lacks almost any emotional words. You'll go days without smiling."

Callan turned on his heel. His feet moved, carrying him away from the threat. *Not this. Not again.* The void hazed over the edges of the room.

She caught his arm before he could escape. He spun as he jerked from her grasp.

"You're never happy. You're never sad. Angry, hurt.

Nothing!" Her foot stomped against the wood flooring. Her eyes blazed. "I *need* to know that you love me."

"Pretty fairytale words for a princess." His voice dripped from his lips. "Which mean more to you than I do."

She smoothed pieces of her hair from her face. The room pulsed in time with his heart—in searing light against red and black shadows. "Are you *actually angry*, Callan?"

"Yeah," he gritted out. He lost the contours of her face. Just light and dark. "Congratulations."

The room narrowed. There wasn't enough air. The pool of acid filled his chest and threatened to overtake him. Callan tried to catch his breath.

"But I—" A pause, then a softer tone. "Sometimes, we need to fight."

"I don't understand." The void pulled at him, but it couldn't take the rage. "When will I be enough for you?"

He slammed his fist into the wall. Cheap drywall cratered around his hand, crumbled to the floor into piles of dust. His knuckles throbbed. Hot liquid oozed across his skin.

"God, Callan—"

He stormed out of their apartment, leaving her behind.

CHAPTER 15

Destination"

A BELIEF THAT JOURNEYS END.

A late-night motorcycle ride was supposed to clear Callan's head. But the void had given its game away. It was actually a sonofabitch. Meant to be a way to find focus in the chaos of battle. Clear mind, calculated shots. Organized retreat.

But for life outside the Corps, its usefulness was limited. Or it should have been lesser. Except it was its own demon. And demons weren't happy being lesser.

It takes her away from me . . . Me from her. Her from me. Goddammit, it's just mixed up. Whispers from the void promised to take it all away. Callan seethed at it, at himself, then realized where he was.

He hadn't been to the cemetery since his deployment. It was a place that stole his breath. He hated the graves that sealed away memories—and people who shouldn't be there.

It's better this way. You knew all along someone like her wouldn't—couldn't—love you. After everything you've done. If she only knew . . .

He pressed his eyes closed and heaved for air.

And even if she knew and found a way to accept you . . . this is where she'd be. Right here, next to the rest of them.

Callan stared at the two headstones. The larger one for Ava Francine Powell Brand, beloved mother, and Elysia Francine Brand, daughter and sister. There had only been ashes to bury. Ashes of what had been a family.

His father's smaller headstone had been erected many years later. But it had just been a formality. Garrett Michael Brand had crawled along in some version of existence, but it had been like watching a corpse twitch. Then eventually stop.

You're a killer. A curse. You can keep hurting her. Or you can save her the pain—because that's all you'll cause her. Save her and end your own suffering as well.

This was *that* voice. The one he tried to drown out so many different ways over the years. Exhaustion had worked best. Pushing his limits on his workouts kept him fit, strong, lucid during the day. Endorphins were the enemy of dark, mind-gnawing demons.

Alcohol had been the worst. It'd almost killed him. Rather, the gun in his hand, when Watts had broken down the door. *That* had almost killed him.

It was the first time the VA doctors told him, "There are options for help."

Options for help? Yeah, just like the last time.

Wind ripped through him, at him. It threatened to tear him apart. This is it, this is how you'll die. Callan fought the terror. There was a high probability his reserve chute would open.

He just needed to have faith. In his training. That it wasn't his time. He still had a mission to complete. This was his team on the ground, counting on him.

To function as their leader.

Map showed a marshy area north of insertion target. *He adjusted his body position and trajectory.* I've got to pull the cord. Pull the cord. Pull it!

Too soon and I end up in those trees. Time it. Just another ten seconds. Nine. Eight.

"Captain, you're too low."

"Stop showing off, you Goddamned—fuck! I swear to God if you're not dead I'm gonna kill you, Brand!"

Two. One. Now! *He yanked the rip cord. The reserve chute shot through the air. Rippled. Then caught. The force pitched him upright.* "Touching down three clicks north of rendezvous point alpha. Go on ahead. I'll catch up."

"No way, Cap. No man left behind. We've still got options if you need help."

His options included marching double time with a broken fibula. For the rest of the exercise, his team picked his ass up off the ground in the mornings. Rayner fashioned a walking splint. Bretty took on his extra gear.

"You got this, Cap. Destination's just up ahead."

Exhaustion bit him to his bone. His leg throbbed. It'd been a tough exercise for even the fittest of his team. But the broken bone was agony; the mental focus required to shut it down wore through his reserves.

"We're gonna get there, Cap, and you'll be golden. Led all us grunts even through the pain."

"Just another day, right, Brand?"

Callan grunted back.

"They never treated me like I was damaged."

I can't give up. I can't let this bullshit beat me.

He sat beside the gravestone. "Mom, I wish I could remember . . . It's like all I've got is your face from old pictures. Dad rarely spoke of you after you were gone. Like the world just sealed you away. I think sometimes I should feel sorrier that you're gone. What kind of son . . ." He hung his head. "This one, I guess. What's left of me." *After my own command, those fuckin' assholes who sit behind the lines and hand down orders like they're some kind of god.*

He seethed. "I knew the limits of my rifle. I knew the terrain. I knew the wind drift. What I didn't fuckin' know was how a Goddamned child . . ." *. . . ended up there. At that moment.*

A blast of cold air swept through the wide, barren lane. The gust filled his lungs, robbing him of the ability to breathe. He turned his head and pulled at the zipper on his jacket, to make sure it was all the way up.

"It could have been Elly. In my nightmares I shoot my own Goddamned sister. Then I wake up and she's dead, and for several, terrible moments, I don't even know if the nightmare was real. Then it finally comes back: she died with you, Mom. But what if one day . . . What if the nightmare just doesn't end?" *What do I do then? Will they lock me away and pump me full of meds until I don't care anymore? Is that the answer?*

He shuddered and leaned back against the grave marker. *I already don't feel much. I just want to be good*

214

enough . . . *for* her. He closed his eyes. *I can't stay. I need to go home. Get back to her.* "Meridian . . ."

She could be leaving you right now.

Callan gritted his teeth. *Why did I yell at her? What's wrong with me?* He banged the back of his head against the granite. Heated, swirling air compressed inside his abdomen. It ached and burned and threatened to erupt through his skin.

Voices yelling like through a tunnel. A fog surrounded the familiar figure of a woman, holding a crying child.

The front door slammed shut.

Callan's head snapped up. His eyes opened. Light seeped over the horizon—the sun rising on a new day.

I'll find a way to adapt. When you reach your limit, you're only at forty percent, Brand.

"There's a destination. It's just up ahead." He swung his leg over his motorcycle. And headed home.

"Desperation"
Is another word for father.

CALLAN PACED THE FLOOR OF THEIR APARTMENT, HIS hands knotted together, separated. Formed tight fists at his sides. He tilted his head—stretching his neck one way, then the other. If Meridian didn't come out of the bathroom in the next thirty seconds, he was going in after her.

Even if he had to break the Goddamned door down. "Meridian!"

His girlfriend emerged from the bathroom. Her features held a sickly pallor. She handed him a long piece of white plastic. In the center of the stick, a small window displayed two pink lines.

He held his breath. "And that means?"

"Yes?" Moist eyes glittered, and a tear rolled down her cheek. His heart thudded and fell. "I don't . . ." She shook her head. "I don't know what to say. I've been on the pill. This isn't supposed to happen."

Callan swallowed, urged his lips to move. When they did, he heard himself say: "Marry me." He gulped down air. *Those are the right words.*

"What?"

"We can apply for a license today. Could be married by next week."

Her jaw dropped, and she stomped one foot. "I don't want to get married just because I'm pregnant!"

That. Was a low blow. "You know that's not what this is. I've been waiting for you and you know it." His whole body vibrated, the room, her. Everything shook. His nails cut into his palms.

"Callan, I—I didn't mean it like that." Her eyes widened and she shuddered. His girlfriend turned around. She went back into the bathroom and shut the door.

He leaned against the wall, then sank to the floor. *A baby.* The idea stirred a strange tumult in his chest. Raider yipped nearby. The fuzzball scratched at the door.

Meridian emerged a few minutes later, looking flushed. Her eyes glassy, she strode toward the door—picking up her purse and keys from the counter on her way.

Callan shook away the void. He leapt to his feet. "Where are you going? If you need something, let me—"

"I need to think."

The tone of her voice stopped him cold; she ran a hand through her hair. The faint sound of her keychain jingling.

"Meridian, this—" He touched her arm.

She pulled away. "I need to think! This wasn't supposed to happen. I can't think. I need to figure out what to—" She spun away, her hand on the doorknob—the simple act set off a series of alarm bells.

Voices yelling. A child crying. The fog swirled and shifted.

The door slammed shut.

His heart froze in his chest. "Don't! Don't go."

"Callan?"

"We'll handle this. But not if you shut me out."

"Who shuts who out?" She turned and drew herself up to her full height. Shoulders square, eyes narrowed to slits. His princess dug in, set her jaw, and stopped just short of an actual fighting stance.

Callan groaned and ran a hand over his face.

"You don't think I know about the nightmares?" Meridian's voice started out low, measured, even. "Or the fits of anger that you hide away from the world?"

His stomach tied itself and his heart into one large, fucked-up knot in his chest. It crowded his lungs and he found it hard to breathe. *No. No, not this.*

"I know why I sometimes wake up alone at night, why you never drink more than one beer, and why you work out like a fiend—as if you'd die if you skipped one day. Babies don't make any of that magically better. If anything, they make it worse."

He glanced around, looking for an escape. But every wall, every corner—she just stripped it all away. And the light was too bright. It burned. *If she leaves, she's not coming back.*

"You don't understand."

"I don't." Her expression wavered; she blinked away tears. "But I've been waiting, all this time, for you to tell me. To give me a chance to understand." She shook her head. "And you've said *not one Goddamned word,* Callan."

He couldn't deny it. He couldn't retreat. The enemy had changed; he couldn't see the threat, but he was fighting for his life all the same.

"These aren't the *pretty words* you often accuse me of wanting to hear because I'm a princess in love with fairy-tales. These are the ugly, terrible, real words that you keep hidden and won't share with anyone. And you need to get them out. Before they fester and warp and change you. Until the damage can't be repaired."

"They're words you never wanted to hear."

"That's not true."

"Isn't it?" A red-tinged haze pulsed in his vision. He pushed at it, willing it to go away. *No, you can't take her.*

"You've asked me hundreds of questions, Meridian. My favorite pizza; my relationship with my parents; did military service run in my family? How much can I bench-press? Do I think flowers have meanings? Do I want children?" He drew in a trembling breath. "Hundreds of questions. But you never asked the guy who told you he was a *sniper* if he killed someone." The rage was too close; it breathed down his neck. "Because you didn't want to deal with it."

"Not true. I knew. When you told me you'd seen combat. The look on your face that day. I knew then. I just could see how much it hurt you." She hugged her arms against her chest. "I thought you'd bring it up. When you were ready. But I—" His girlfriend closed her eyes and turned. She leaned one temple against the door.

"How long have you known?"

"About the PTSD? A while now. I woke up one night and you weren't there. I went to find you; you were on the balcony. Hunched over the rail. Every muscle in your body looked like it was strung so tight you might just snap in half." A tear trickled down the side of her face. "I called your name, but you didn't hear me. And you were shaking. I figured you were out there because you weren't ready"—she wiped at her eyes—"to talk about it with me. I wanted it to be your choice."

Callan shoved harder against the void. "It's not all the time. And they over-diagnose veterans with the disorder."

"I looked it up. When you didn't say anything the next morning. They're textbook PTSD symptoms."

Callan let out a long breath. He'd looked it up, too, determined to prove the doctors wrong. But for some reason, when she said it . . . with that look on her face . . .

Carrying his child.

"I can't do this, Callan. I'm scared and I need you. Our child will need you. You're its father."

Oh God. I know what it was like, living with, being raised by, a specter of a father. How can I let my child—

He choked and forced his tongue to move, to say something, anything: "If I agreed to see someone. To work through it. If you'd go with me?"

She bowed her head. "You're a wonderful man."

"With over a hundred confirmed enemy kills, Meridian."

She gasped, and her keys clanged against the wood floor.

"Please. Don't leave. I'd *never* abandon you or our child. I swear."

"Callan, I never thought you'd . . . I *love* you. I want a life with you. I want us to have a family together. I do."

"I thought I could deal with it. On my own. But I guess . . . I haven't. I can't." The nothingness hummed all around him. It pulled him to his knees. "I can't even tell you . . ."

He heard footsteps, and then she was kneeling beside him, pulling him into her arms. He felt her tears on his cheek. He wrapped his arms around her waist and buried his face into her shoulder.

"Just. Don't go."

"Grief" and "Forgiveness"
One of these is abundant. The other is missing.

SIX MONTHS LATER

Callan stood in the corner of the small, gray-painted office. He wanted to run, to blunt the rawness. The ache. Meridian stepped into the room. Her eyes flitted around, and she lowered her rounded body onto the sofa.

"Where's Callan?"

The therapist, Justine, gestured in his direction.

His fiancée. She allowed him to call her that—in public. Or at least in front of the doctors who'd become a regular part of their lives. Meridian turned, met his gaze, and straightened in her seat. She offered him a small smile.

"Here is a rather factual account of his background. It's what the military had on file. It's cataloged in chronological order. He wants you to read it, first. Then we're going to try to answer some of your questions."

Justine stood. She was a middle-aged woman with a kindly face, and she wore a wedding ring on her left hand. Callan tried not to seethe with bitterness.

She handed a folder to Meridian.

"Thank you."

"I'll warn you, now. Even a fact-based account . . . it's not pleasant. In any way. Except that he's survived. And here, trying to heal."

Callan crossed his arms against his chest. These doctors made him want to jump out the window. This one sincere enough, but the nonstop optimism and praise still made him cringe.

Silence filled the room like a lead balloon. It felt heavy and took up all the available air. Callan started to count, to measure his breaths. *No. Sit in it. It sucks, but it won't kill you.*

Meridian looked up from the pages; she glanced his direction, then back at the therapist.

"H-he mentioned, after the first time we were . . . intimate, not wanting me to be taken away from him. As a reason why . . ." She frowned. "Why he couldn't say how he felt about me."

"Callan?"

He groused and looked toward the window. Bits of sun peeked through gray blinds. The faint smell of smoke wafted in. But he knew it was a lie.

"Meridian's asking you a reasonable question. Can you answer it?"

He shut his eyes. His skin smoldered and burned. *There's no enemy here.*

"Start with the factual details." The older woman's voice grated every syllable to shreds.

"It's in the report."

"OK. Can you help us find the pieces? How they fit together for you."

"December seventeenth, 2002. February twenty-sixth, 2008. June seventh, 2015." His voice warbled in his throat.

"I don't see—" Meridian looked up at him. Her eyebrows knit together. "The first two dates?"

Callan threw the therapist a look. "It's there."

Pages flipped and, finally: "Ah. Here!" Justine held up a page, stood, and handed it to Meridian.

222

She chewed her lip as she read. "So, his—"

"You need to go speak to him." The woman's voice was nauseatingly patient. "Make eye contact."

"All right." Meridian struggled to her feet and moved across the room. She placed her hand on his forearm. Her touch soothed at the desire to peel away his own skin. She peered up at him. "You lost your mother and sister in a terrible accident."

He gave her a nod and held her gaze.

"You lost your father to cancer."

Callan wet his lips and managed to grit out, "Yeah."

"Your childhood friend—was killed by an IED. Just a few meters away from you."

There are no words for that.

A tight smile. "It hurt. So much, when my adoptive father died. I was about the same age as you were, when your father passed away."

He brushed a tear from her cheek. "I remember . . . feeling hurt, too." Something filled and warmed his chest. Instead of numbing the pain, an ache razed his insides. She pulled his hand into hers. "Shared life experiences?"

Her mouth tilted up. "Yeah. I guess we found one."

Their hands folded together. Her fingers laced with his.

"But I still don't understand. Why? Why do you think you'll lose me?"

He released her hand, crossed his arms. He looked away.

"Callan? Talk to me. *Please.*"

The ache turned into a gaping, sucking wound inside

his chest. Haze, no longer gray but tinged with color, offered to take it. He shook his head.

Meridian's hands flitted across his cheeks and tilted his head toward her. He swallowed.

"I took others."

"You took others?"

Callan pressed his eyes closed. "They were enemies, targets, threats. But to someone else, they were a son or a father or a husband." *Or their little girl.* "And they never went home again."

"But you didn't—"

"God. Or the universe. Knew what I would do."

"So, it's your punishment? That you lost people close to you? And so . . . if you don't let people get close . . ." Her features tightened. "But that's—that's not true! That's not why . . . Bad things happen sometimes. Things we don't deserve. And sometimes, amazing things happen. And we don't deserve that either." Her palms cupped his face. "We take the bad *with the good*. Like how that creep followed me home. And you protected me. I was so scared, but we became friends."

"You're going to be my friend now, aren't you?" Callan turned his back to her as he fastened his pants. Dressed, he headed toward the coffee.

"You could try to escape, but I'm pretty determined."

"You were so closed, but I could see . . ." Her mouth curved. "Your kindness."

I thought I was saving you. But all this time . . .

"You're going to be a wonderful father."

Her thumb brushed something wet across his cheek. Was that . . . him?

She pulled him into a kiss; he bristled at first, then decided, therapist be damned, he wanted to kiss Meridian.

"Don't worry, Brand." She smiled through so many tears. "You're still a big bad Marine to the rest of the world. But with me, just be you. You're *enough*."

"Hm." He relaxed into her embrace, his forehead brushing hers as he moved pieces of hair stuck to her cheek.

"You *will* need to keep some of that intimidating glare for when our daughter starts to date."

Callan shut his eyes. "She can date when I'm dead."

Callan stood outside the therapist's door. Waiting. He tilted his head, resting it on the panel. His practiced ears picked out the two female voices on the other side.

"He's been trying, at home. But he still gives me blank stares at odd times."

"I know it doesn't help to say 'that's normal,' but it will be for a while."

"It hurts when feeling the baby kick, or seeing her on the ultrasound, doesn't seem to register. These are important moments. He deserves some happiness. Even if he doesn't believe it."

"It's not an overnight solution," the older women's voice said with a sigh. "Even from here. It's great he's trying at home. But while we always hope for improvement and healing to come quickly, he has a lot to deal with. Past, present, and future."

"I know. But he's committed to it. He keeps proving that."

Callan let out a slow breath.

"Yes. You've been a catalyst for him, in many ways. The records the VA sent over show that doctors advised him on four separate occasions to seek some sort of psychiatric treatment. And he shut down the suggestion almost as soon as the words were uttered."

Callan stuffed his hands in his pockets. *Everyone has trauma. I could manage mine. Until I couldn't.*

"I see."

"He has a remarkable service record. I see far too many well-decorated servicemen. But even in such company, his record is exceptional. I like to see real-life heroes find some stability and happiness."

"Thank you. I do, too. But I—I still have so many questions."

Meridian . . . Callan closed his eyes. He could see her face in his mind. Her blue-green eyes held a light and warmth his never had.

"Meridian, there are a lot of tough days ahead. You might want to find your own support group."

The sound of shuffling.

"Even if you're not interested, or able to keep the romantic aspect of your lives—"

More shuffling. Some mumbling Callan couldn't make out. His lungs squeezed. He needed more air.

"Sometimes—" Meridian's voice broke. "It's just hard."

"No one would blame you for . . ." Justine's voice faded for a moment. "Of course I hope you can. But it's not right to feel trapped."

Callan turned his head; he quieted his own breathing.

"Anyway. A support group for wives and girlfriends of soldiers with PTSD would help you find the right balance and keep perspective."

"Thank you. For the advice. I do have one question."

Callan straightened.

"Is it . . . possible? Likely? That as he stops this, uh—"

"Disassociation."

"Yes, as he stops disassociating, and realizes or regains his full emotional spectrum, that he'd realize . . ."

"That he doesn't really love you?"

Callan dispelled all the air in his lungs; his heart squeezed to the point of pain.

"I know it's a terrible thing to worry about."

He could picture the strain on her features, her hands patting her stomach as if she were trying to comfort their child—instead of herself.

No. Tell her no.

"Anything is possible."

He groaned.

"But I highly doubt that will be the case between you and Callan. In fact, I gave him a mission. Which he accepted."

"A mission?"

"He's supposed to be writing down words. The words and feelings specific to his relationship with you. How you met, how your relationship developed. And evolved. He's writing me a report. We'll go through the words he chooses in future sessions."

It's strange. How many words I have for her.

First.

Determined.

Stubborn.

Breathtaking.

And how they compare to the ones for myself.

Jealous.

Unromantic.

Unlovable.

Desperate.

"Oh." Meridian's voice brought him back to the present.

"He fell in love with you when he blunted everything else. And detached from almost everyone else. I expect his report to be an interesting study." The faint thud of footsteps. "Do you still think you need to worry?"

"Even if"—she took a loud breath—"he doesn't love me, I want him to get better. To bond with his daughter."

"And what about you, Meridian?"

Callan stared at the door. Raw and razed and present. A crucial moment—when *he* wasn't the one with his finger on the trigger.

"Me?" His girlfriend's voice pitched higher. Then: "Hmmmm." It warmed and lowered.

He held his breath.

"I decided some time ago. He's the only one who suits me."

CHAPTER 16

"Love"

IS ANOTHER WORD FOR FORGIVENESS. AND THE COURAGE TO CREATE SOMETHING NEW.

"Callan?" Meridian panted, breathless. He darted upright, instantly awake. His heart thudded loudly in his ears.

"You OK?"

"Contractions. I—I'm not sure, but—I think we should time them."

"Roger that." He launched the stopwatch function on his phone. "When do I—"

"Uhhhhnnnng. Noooow." Pant. Pant.

He hit the button to start the timer. Meridian's hand found his on top of the comforter. "Do you need anything? I'll get water. Staying hydrated is the best thing you can do."

"O-K." She puffed the letters and held her swollen belly.

Callan gained his feet; he didn't bother throwing his shorts on before exiting their room. He moved with haste to the kitchen, grabbed a water bottle from the fridge, and hurried back.

Just as he sat down on her side of the bed, Meridian cried out. Raider stuck to her side.

"Breathe," he told her, and hit the button on the stopwatch. "Remember your breathing exercises."

She puffed and panted. The pained expression lifted from her face. Callan opened the water bottle and handed it to her. She gave him a lopsided smile. "Where is it?"

"Hmm?"

"Where's the bracelet? Put it on. Or get some ice." She shook her head. "Focus and stay with me. I need you, Callan." Her breaths puffed with exertion. "...time the contractions."

"Did I fade?" He felt the urge to punch something. "Dammit."

"It's OK. You're safe. You're safe to be here with me."

"I know."

"Knowing and feeling—"

"Aren't the same thing. I'm here, with you. And *she* will be, soon?"

"I hope so. I'm so tired of being pregnant. She's already a week late."

"Drink your water. I'll call the doctor."

Callan dialed and got the after-hours service. They paged the doctor on call. He heard her groan again; he took a breath and hit the button on the stopwatch. Seven minutes between contractions.

He looked at the bracelet on his wrist. It was something Meridian had bought him after a suggestion from the therapist. A simple leather piece with an intricately carved silver feather charm. He ran a finger over the ridges. The texture was supposed to remind him that this was the present.

A present where he was about to become a father. A present where an amazing woman was about to give birth— a woman who loved him and would, hopefully, someday *actually* marry him.

His phone rang. "Brand," he answered.

"Mr. Brand, this is Dr. Stuart. I have a message that your fiancée, a patient of Dr. Peng, is in labor?"

"Affirmative. Contractions approximately seven minutes apart."

"And these contractions aren't small, hiccup-like, but substantial, lasting for—"

"The last one lasted two minutes."

"And she's in week forty-one. Let's get Meridian to the hospital, and we'll make sure that baby comes out. Sound good?"

"Yeah."

"See you in about an hour."

CALLAN FOUND HIS FIANCÉE, HELPED HER THROW ON A loose maternity dress, and deposited her into her little Civic. Their bags had been packed in the trunk for a few weeks already.

It wasn't a long drive, about fifteen minutes at night with no traffic. He parked the car in the parking garage; Meridian's hand came up to rest on his forearm. Her fingers toyed with the feather on the bracelet.

"I'm here. I want to be here. I want to meet our daughter."

"I know. And I love you. I'm not being critical. I just know." She smiled with bleary eyes. "You need this. But it won't be easy. Just keep trying."

He took her hand and lifted their joined fingers to his lips. "I could say the same to you."

"I know it won't be easy. She's your child after all. Nothing's going to be easy ever again."

Callan raised an eyebrow. "The stubborn, difficult genes are from your side."

"They're definitely yours."

As soon as they entered the hospital and signed in, "not easy" began. Meridian had to fill out registration forms in between contractions. Because they weren't married, she had to sign some extra HIPAA forms for him to be allowed in the room with her. And even then, when the doctor arrived—he was asked to step out.

She would fill him in as soon as he was allowed back inside. But it was stupid and tedious and wouldn't have been a factor if she'd just married him!

"Not easy" slipped quickly into "irritating" and, over the dark hours of morning, changed into "difficult."

And then her fuckin' brother showed up.

Callan stood in the hallway, just outside her private room in the labor-and-delivery wing of the hospital. The epidural had allowed his fiancée to get a bit of sleep. But he needed air; his joints ached to move. And yet he hadn't made it farther than the hall.

Just in case.

A loud cough. Callan's head whipped; his eyes shot open. He glanced around his immediate area. The corner of the wall jutted out and stabbed his shoulder. *I fell asleep standing up. Ugh.* He rubbed a hand over his face and yawned.

"You're the neighbor. The Marine," a deep voice said. Callan's shoulders tightened. His eyes found the speaker.

A tall, aristocratic-looking man raised a light-colored eyebrow and glared down his turned-up nose. He smoothed hair the same color as Meridian's into place.

"Repeat that?" Callan rose to his full height. But the man still towered over him.

"She lives across the hall from you."

"Lived there. She's my fiancée now." He eyed the stranger. Gray button-down, finely pressed; the sleeves brushed his wrists. A navy linen jacket. With cufflinks.

"Who are you?"

Eyes the same blue as chips of ice.

"No, I know who you are. You're Holden Cavallier. I recognize you. I also know she didn't call you."

"No. She texted. I'm not the bad guy. Our family is a bit much sometimes. But she and I—"

"Why are you *here*?"

"My parents insist the child is a Cavallier. I don't personally give a shit, but they can be . . . intrusive. I came to persuade the father to take responsibility."

"You've gotta be fuckin' kidding me. The 'unmarried' part is a technicality."

Holden visibly bristled. "Not a technicality. Maybe where you come from. But not in *our* family."

"Where I come from? You have some nerve."

"Yes. I do, don't I?" His mouth twisted into a smug-looking grin. The urge to punch it off his face bordered on *need*. It seized Callan's arm where it connected to his shoulder. "Just leave."

"Not before I see my sister."

"I kept asking her to marry me. The 'unmarried' part is her doing. Not mine."

Holden sighed. "Figures. She still has that damned rebellious streak. I keep thinking she might grow up. One of these days."

"Hm."

"Have you considered"—that icy gaze met his—"what her daughter will be like?"

"Yeah." Callan clutched the feather charm on his bracelet. *Stubborn. Maddening. Difficult. Amazing. Just like her mother.*

Silence stretched the length of the hallway.

A nurse appeared, one he might have seen before. She smiled and pointed at Meridian's room across the corridor.

"Mr. Brand, Meridian's asking for you."

MERIDIAN HELD OUT HER HAND AND TOOK HIS; SHE threaded their fingers together and pointed with the other hand to something that looked a bit like an EKG. "It's a fetal monitor."

Two separate sections displayed real-time data in the form of lines with various peaks and valleys.

"The bottom line measures how powerful the contractions are. The upper one is Elysia's heartbeat."

Callan nodded.

"The doctor is monitoring the baby for heart acceleration and deceleration patterns."

"Why?"

"Her descent has stopped progressing like they'd hoped. Breaking the amniotic sac didn't result in faster dilation." She let out a ragged breath. The top line began to climb.

"Contraction?"

"I can't really feel it."

He watched the bottom line dip, then return to its peak; the top line stair-stepped back down from its high.

"The doctors started me on Pitocin to try to get her to re-engage." Her fingers tightened around his hand.

Callan watched the lines move up and down. "But she's OK."

"Yes, her heartbeat is fine. Which means she's fine. They're just watching for any sign that she becomes . . . not fine."

"How would we know?"

"The contractions should correspond with the small dips in her heart rate."

Callan took in the patterns in the data displayed on-screen. Sure enough, just before the contraction line began to climb, their daughter's heart rate dipped and then quickly returned to its variable, sawtooth pattern.

"And if something happens?"

"Surgery. Cesarean section. They won't let anything

happen to her. It's just"—a tear traced a glistening path down her cheek—"taking longer."

"You're crying."

"I'm tired. And I want to meet her. And I don't want you to worry."

He growled as his stomach tied itself into a hot, acidic knot. "You can't protect me, Meridian. I'm fine. I'm here."

She yawned and seemed to sigh at the same time. "Tell me how you're feeling."

"Exhausted."

"Physical, not emotional. Give me emotional."

He tried to disentangle his hand, but she wouldn't let go. "Not now. It's too much."

"Yes, now. You're stronger than this."

"Irritated."

"That just covers up what you really feel. Dig deeper."

He yanked from her grasp and turned away. But he could still see her in his mind: sweat-slicked blond hair, weary blue-green eyes. One of those terrible hospital smocks. IV in her left arm, wires around her belly, black lines threading out of the neck of her gown. *And she's worried about me. Fuck this.*

Callan ran both hands through his hair. "I can't do this with you right now. Your fuckin' brother showed up and tells me I need to *take responsibility*. And how my child is part of *their* family! And then you—you try to protect me from what's going on, but give me some tired line about being stronger." The room trembled, but there was no haze this time.

He pivoted to face her. "I can't do this with you right now."

"I will get up off this table and make you, Callan Brand. This is *your* daughter. No one can or will take that away from you." Her gaze met his; that stubborn chin jutted out. "I won't lie; you have a right to be angry that I kept you from being treated like the husband and father. That was my mistake—but I certainly didn't do it with the intent to hurt you like this."

"I know."

"Now, stop using anger. I know it's powerful, it makes you feel in control. But you can't connect. Try."

Callan glanced at the monitor, watching the lines rise and fall. "I'm anxious. I'm—I'm worried that I could lose you both. And that thought"—he sank down in the chair beside her bed—"is terrifying."

He bent forward and laid his head on her chest. She slipped her fingers in and out of his hair.

"We'll be all right."

CALLAN WOKE SOMETIME LATER; HIS NECK ACHED AND throbbed. Meridian snored lightly on the hospital bed. The monitor beeped. Another contraction. He watched the indicator line for his daughter's heartbeat. From what he could tell, everything looked like the same pattern as before: a slight dip in heart rate just before the contraction. Lots of peaks and valleys indicating a variable heart rate.

The room began to fade; the lines all blurred together. He shook it away. *No, focus. You can't keep running away.*

A nurse stole quietly into the room. "You're awake."

"Yeah."

"She's still out?"

"Affirmative."

"We'll let her sleep a bit longer."

Callan nodded.

The monitor beeped again. Another contraction. Meridian's brow dipped in her sleep. Callan glanced up at the line on the monitor. And the tingling sensation along the back of his neck burned. He blinked. *It doesn't follow the pattern.* He turned to see the nurse—about to walk out of the room. "Nurse."

She opened the door and stepped into the hall.

"Nurse!"

The woman stopped; she turned. "Yes?"

"The heart rate dipped after the contraction. Not before."

She let the door shut and quickly returned to Meridian's bedside. "It's only a problem if it repeats."

The nurse made some notations on her tablet. "The epidural injection will be wearing off soon. I'm going to put in a call for an anesthesiologist. STAT, just in case."

"Just in case of—"

The fetal monitor beeped. Callan and the nurse watched . . .

The baby's—his daughter's—heart rate dipped again. Meridian moaned.

"I'll get the doctor right away."

"What does this—"

"It's not my place to say, but if the doctor makes the decision, it could mean an emergency C-section."

He blinked, and the room swarmed with people. Dr. Peng arrived, along with several nurses. An anesthesiologist. Meridian was patted awake. She sought him out with her eyes from across the room.

Words were said. Her face paled. The doctor looked at him. "We're going to put her under. The fetus is showing signs of distress. It could still recover, or the distress could get worse. At this point, she's been in labor long enough— with her permission, we're erring on the side of caution."

Callan nodded. "Can I go with her?"

The older woman shook her head. "Being under general anesthetic, we don't allow partners or family members to attend the surgery. I'm sorry, but you'll have to leave now."

"I want to stay. Until she goes into surgery. I'm the father."

"We aim to have her in surgery within thirty minutes." She put one hand on his forearm and pointed toward the door. "You need to step out. We'll have a nurse bring you an update."

He gritted his teeth. "Fine. But I'll speak to her before I go." He snarled at the doctor; people moved out of his way.

Callan took Meridian's hand and knelt down. He kissed her forehead.

"Marines never say die."

She smiled with bleary eyes. "Neither do fairy princesses."

"Mine doesn't."

"And our daughter is half Marine, half fairy princess."

He squeezed her hand. "Elysia and I will be here when you wake up."

Tears came to her eyes. "I love you."

He might have said it then. The words lifted but stuck to his tongue. He licked his lips. Callan tried to force the sounds to manifest. But his window of opportunity was too short. She closed her eyes and sank into the pillow. A nurse touched his arm.

"The general anesthetic has taken hold; we have to move her now."

He nodded; he wiped the tears from her cheek and left the room.

CHAPTER 17

"Heroism"

IS IN THE EYE OF THE BEHOLDER.

Callan wanted to sit in a dark, quiet spot, to focus on his breathing. If there was one thing a former sniper could do well, it was wait. Patiently. Quietly. Without a sound. Barely a movement. Just him, a quiet mind, and his breath.

Waiting for Meridian and his daughter to emerge from surgery could have been the simplest thing she'd ever asked him to do.

Except she'd managed to text Nora before they carted her off. The only time she could have managed it was when he was talking to Dr. Peng. And Callan knew, when he saw their friends in the waiting room: his princess was too stubborn to die this day.

"Callan, how're you holding up?" Nora's hazel eyes turned down at the corners. She sat in the chair next to him and patted his arm.

"Meridian's in surgery." He focused on the floor tile; the

thin lines formed crisp edges around the toe of his boot. "A nurse will provide updates."

"The text she sent just asked us to come wait with you."

Breathe in. Hold for two seconds. "They said she'd be in surgery within thirty minutes. The procedure won't take long."

"Sounds like a great time for coffee." Watts clapped him on the back.

Callan glanced up. The walking, always-talking irritant leaned down and gave him a grin.

"I don't need a pep talk."

"Good, 'cause I'm terrible at 'em. I just really want some coffee."

"You two go on." Nora offered him another one of her sad smiles.

She texted them because she doesn't want me to be alone. He stood from his seat in the dark corner of the room, shoved his hands in his pockets, and trudged after his friend.

They crossed the auditorium-sized waiting room and headed toward the café. Sun streamed in through the glass front walls of the building; he hadn't even been sure it was daytime. "You want to talk about something. Your ruse is obvious."

"Eh, you caught me. You know she's going to be all right. Yeah?"

Watts stepped up to the counter, held two fingers in the air, then pointed to the coffee maker on the other side of the baked goods.

Watts pressed a steaming paper cup into his palm; the heat bit his skin. Callan met his friend's gaze.

"Meridian and your daughter. This isn't some cosmic 'avenge the lives we took on the battlefield' thing. You know that, right?"

Callan looked away. *Dammit. I don't want to deal with this right now.*

"See, I have this theory."

Callan ran his thumb over the feather charm. The ridges were warm from resting against his skin. *Be present. Listen.* He shifted from one toe to the other—and concentrated on the feel of his boots against his feet. Where they rubbed.

"I think we live our lives in boxes." Watts spilled into a seat outside the little café.

"Boxes?"

"Yeah. Sit." He gestured at the chair across from him. "We create our own box, ya know. To suit a purpose. So we can be who and what we imagine ourselves to be."

"I don't follow." Callan folded himself to fit in the metal chair.

"It's like you put up these walls you can't see through, so you can make the inside work however you want it to. Like, if you wanted to add horizontal gravity, you could add magnets to the outside of one wall. And rig the box."

"You're not making any sense."

"The box you built allows you to be this tough-guy Marine. Almost superhuman. You made the walls so thick, you didn't have to feel anything. You didn't have to let anyone in, either. And according to your rules in your box—

that made you successful. Complete. Admirable." Watts took a sip of his coffee and blanched. One hand waved at his face—like it could stop molten lava from destroying his insides.

"Hot?"

Watts flipped him the bird. "See, but in my world, in my box, your existence was lonely and unhappy. Powerless, to an extent. Because the way I rigged my box to work, it's the people I make a difference to that matter."

Callan flat out didn't know what to say.

"Look. I'm not saying you're anything less than a hero—to this country. To the Corps. But, man, you've gotta be a hero to that woman in there who'd give her own life to bring your kid into the world. And you've gotta learn how to be one to your daughter."

Callan stared at the cup in front of him. Steam rose from the dark-brown liquid, carrying the warm, rich smell of coffee with it. *When will they tell me something about Meridian, and—*

"You need a new fuckin' box. Instead of how many miles you can march with a rucksack and all that stuff we did in the Corps—you've got to build a new structure of what makes you successful. What makes you feel *full*—full of life and love and joy and pain. And yeah, sometimes ya gotta fight and feel pain. To experience the wonders and the joy."

"You were right the first time," Callan said, and rose to his feet.

"What?"

"You really suck at pep talks."

"Eh. You got the message." Watts stood and grabbed his friend's shoulder.

"To sum up: stop being a Marine, you dick, and be a man."

Callan shoved him away. He took his coffee and headed back toward his corner of the waiting room.

"She's already been changing you, you know. I can almost tolerate you now."

"Maybe Nora will work some magic and make you tolerable someday."

"I wouldn't hold out a lot of hope if I were you," Watts said with his patented shit-eating grin.

"I don't."

CALLAN MANAGED TO MAKE IT BACK TO THE WAITING room and sit down for a whole five minutes before a nurse emerged from a door, carrying a tablet—and called his name.

"Callan Brand?"

He stood and crossed the small space in a couple of strides. His nails dug into the skin of his palm. Callan couldn't catch his breath; instead, air came in short, sharp gasps.

"Your daughter was born about eight minutes ago. She's with the NICU, but her Apgar scores are normal. They're keeping her in a warmer while the surgeons finish up with mom."

Callan nodded. Relief razed the back of his throat.

"She's a healthy eight pounds one ounce. Nineteen inches long. As soon as mom is ready to be moved into the recovery room, we'll bring you back so you can meet your daughter."

"How's Meridian?"

"She's doing fine. It shouldn't be much longer."

"Thanks."

She smiled. "You're welcome. I'll be back in a few minutes."

Callan met Holden's eyes from across the waiting room. He nodded and tilted his head. Meridian's brother stood— the man looked like he was seven feet tall—and crossed the room in short order.

"Elysia's OK. She was born a few minutes ago. They're just stitching Meridian up; they'll let me see her in the recovery room. Once we get to the hospital room, you can come up. I'll text you."

"Thanks. You need my phone number?"

"I've got it."

"You recognized me and you have my phone number." His mouth pressed into a severe line.

"Reconnaissance. My daughter's future boyfriends stand no chance."

Holden stared at him for a moment before his face split into a grin. "My sister's always been a little different. Leave it to her to find someone like you."

Callan shrugged. "We suit one another. If I have my way, I'll get to find out if we can make it a lifetime."

"You think she ever quits?"

God, I hope not. He shoved his hands in his pockets.

"Your daughter's name is Elysia?"

"Elysia Yvonne Brand. The first name is in honor of my sister."

"Cavallier. Did she tell you why Yvonne?"

He squared his shoulders. "Adoptive mother. And Brand's going on that birth certificate."

"Mr. Brand?" the nurse called out. "Ah, good. They're bringing Meridian into the recovery room. You can come on back."

A dour-looking Holden Cavallier glared at his future brother-in-law.

Callan offered him a small salute, and followed the nurse through the door marked "Restricted Access." He pointed at the sign and mouthed, "Only family allowed."

Then left the red-faced uninvited guest behind.

THE RECOVERY ROOM WAS MADE OF CONCRETE AND tile—and partitioned with fabric curtains. A few pieces of medical monitoring equipment sat about; there was space to wheel in a hospital gurney, and a single, uncomfortable plastic chair.

Callan couldn't sit. He had to pace. After a few minutes that felt like an hour, a nurse arrived. The woman held a tiny human swaddled in a blanket; a pink-and-blue striped hat covered its head. Her head.

His daughter.

Callan froze. He couldn't breathe. The woman held the

infant out, toward him. As if he should be allowed to touch such a small, precious . . . life.

"Mr. Brand?"

Callan nodded and stared at the newborn. Her eyes closed tight, her face flushed and red. Full, round cheeks met at tiny, perfect lips—beneath a petite version of her mother's nose.

The nurse stepped closer; she brought his arm up and worked the sleeping infant in between his forearm and chest. The chair came up behind him. Callan sat and held his daughter. And just felt . . . happy. To watch her breathe.

He couldn't have been there long before they wheeled a pale, groggy version of his princess into the room. Someone told them that Elysia should try to nurse, so Callan found his legs, stood, and introduced their daughter to her mom.

"She's incredible." Meridian held out her arms. The newborn lifted her eyelids as she was passed to her mother; Callan caught just a flash of dark blue.

He watched as his princess held their daughter against her chest. And was amazed when the little thing parted its lips and attached itself to her mom's nipple. Meridian winced.

"You OK?"

She nodded. "I'm alive. Itchy and foggy and tired with the most adorable little snapping turtle attached to my chest. But. She's finally here. And they said she's fine. We caught it—you caught it—probably as soon as her position started compressing the umbilical cord. We may not have—"

"It's OK. She's here. She's fine. You're fine. That's all I need."

She smiled; her eyes drifted closed. "Hmm. Did you ever think, when we first met, that we'd be here? With a beautiful daughter and a whole lifetime ahead of us?"

"I knew the first time I saw you I wanted to get you pregnant."

"You're terrible."

"You were dripping wet with a see-through blouse. And cold. It really was all I could do not to offer to warm you up. In a stalker sort of way."

She opened one eye. "Instead, you barked at me to buy an umbrella. Not the best pickup line."

"It worked."

She laughed. "I guess it did."

"So, when are you going to marry me?"

"When are you going to give me a real proposal?"

"That's what this has been about? You still need pretty words."

She blinked open both eyes; Elysia whimpered as her mom adjusted her position. "That's not why. But pretty words are nice. And you now have two fairy princesses to deal with, so maybe you should reapply to Prince Charming school. You're going to have to up your game, Brand."

"You said I was too stubborn to change."

"But you have." She held their daughter, her eyes completely focused on the tiny being. "Bit by bit. Haven't you?"

"Hm. Who knew fairy princesses could out-stubborn a Marine?"

Meridian giggled.

"If I propose, will you accept this time?"

She gave him a look. "It's not much of a proposal if there's no suspense."

"I'm just going to kidnap you and take you to the JP at this rate."

"You still need me to say yes at some point. I'm pretty sure."

"Well. Is this romantic enough? This place?"

"You're asking if a partitioned-off hospital warehouse of a recovery space with me half asleep, lying on a gurney in a reusable gown and holding your newborn daughter—is the right place and time to propose?"

Callan took her hand and knelt beside her. Tears sprang to her eyes. "Don't you dare." But her mouth turned up into a fragile smile and tears coursed down her cheeks—like the rainwater on the day they'd first met . . .

And he knew. This was the crucial moment.

Epilogue: "Forever"

IT ISN'T EASY, BUT IT'S WORTH THE PRICE OF ADMISSION.

Callan stared at the woman standing at the other end of a long aisle. In a small church, with a sprinkling of friends and a few family members. A sharp clap on the back of his shoulder jarred him from his thoughts.

"Well, I have to say, you finally made it. Took the long route, as usual. Idiot. But you're finally making an honest woman out of her."

"It's been a mutual . . . progression."

"Well, if you'd waited a few more years, your daughter could have been a flower girl. But Nora seems to be enjoying toddler snuggles. Maybe it'll tide her over for a little longer." He sighed and shot Callan a guilty look. "She wants to 'start a family,' she says."

"It'll probably make her want one that much more." Callan bared his teeth in a wicked grin.

Watts's features fell. His lip curled up in a sour-looking snarl. "Great."

Music started, and Meridian's brother, who had become

a new addition to their daily life soon after Elysia was born —took her arm to lead her down the aisle.

As they neared the front of the church, shining blue-green eyes met his gaze. He smiled.

"Last chance to run for it." Watts dug an elbow into his rib.

"No way," Callan hissed under his breath, and stepped forward.

"Who gives this bride away?"

"I do." Holden's ice-blue eyes darted his way; jaw tight, he nodded, then looked back at the priest.

Her brother hadn't been excited that Meridian had had their child "out of wedlock," but had to accept that there were other issues at hand.

The birth of their daughter had been . . . crazy. Stressful. Miraculous. And the first year of her life was the hardest thing Callan had ever done. It wasn't the sleepless nights, the crying, or the diaper changes. Those were hard, but nothing like boot camp. Or sitting quietly in a swamp for several hours, waiting, watching for the enemy—hoping insects couldn't actually eat him alive.

It was the work of . . . coping with loss. Forgiving himself. Believing he was allowed to have a better life; and learning to have faith.

Emotionally draining and mentally grueling—Meridian made the journey with him, holding his hand when it became too much. And calling him on his bullshit when he tried to shut down.

And his reward was standing here, beside him. Their daughter babbling and fussing in the front aisle, his friend offering to help him escape, his disapproving brother-in-law glaring at him from across the room.

He was right where he wanted to be.

"I, Callan Brand, take you, Meridian Daly Cavallier, to be my lawfully wedded wife. To love, honor, and cherish you for the rest of my days." His hand didn't shake when he fitted the ring on her finger. But his voice trembled just a bit when he went off script, raised her hand to his lips, and said:

"Meridian, my wife . . ."

She met his gaze and moved her head like she was trying to shake it. "Not yet."

But this was the crucial moment . . .

"I love you."

Thank You for Reading!

Would you do me a favor, And please leave a review?

I really appreciate that you took the time and took a chance on **Losing My Breath**. I'm excited to hear what you thought of it!

It would mean a lot to me if you would please leave an honest review for the book. 🩶

https://www.amazon.com/review/create-review/?ie=UTF8&channel=glance-detail&asin=B0C8HQCFZB

Thank you so much!
~Rose

Afterword

I think I'll just leave this where we started:

"One of the most important things you can do on this earth
is to let people know they are not alone."

— SHANNON L. ALDER

Thank you for reading.
All my love,
J. Rose Black

Acknowledgments

Thank you so so much to Mallory Rock of Rock Solid Book Design - for the amazing cover! www.RockSolidBookDesign.com

Thank you to Coley Jen for betareading the first, second, and nineteenth versions! LOL

Thank you - Mellie & Mr. King for all your support on this one…and the self-publishing adventure in general. <3

Thank you to Nina, my developmental editor! Even though I don't always like you, I love you.

Thank you to Elizabeth, my everything-else editor! For making everything perfect down to the last period. And putting up with my neuroses.

Thank you to Nora, my launch team coordinator! You're dynamite!

Thank you to my fabulous launch team, for being fabulously fantastic!

Thank you to Warisha, who designed the most amazing logos a person could have never imagined. (so cute!)

Thank you to Diane for her mad embroidery skills!

Thank you, Rachel, for your help with all kinds of things! (and stuff)

Thank you to Ginger for your mad ad design skills!

Thank you, Tessa, for all the website help!

Thank you to everyone who took the time to read this book. Please tell me what you thought! I'd love to hear from you!

About the Author

An award-winning and multi-genre author, J. Rose Black weaves stories about obsession, redemption, and the transcendental power of love. From her early days writing fanfiction for a passionate following of international readers, to crafting novels with her own characters, Rose has always been drawn to broody protectors and plucky, no-nonsense women ready to fight for what they believe in.

When Rose isn't immersed in her latest manuscript, she's working in cybersecurity, thwarting the next generation of internet bad guys. Out of the office, she's #Shipping with friends over her favorite couples, heading to the gym to battle the evil that is Unmovable Baby Weight, or complaining about her husband's addiction to 3D printing. Also: nagging her children to eat something other than cheese.

To learn more about Rose's stories and the characters and worlds visited inside this book, check out her website: https://jroseblack.com or on socmed:

facebook.com/jrose.black.5

x.com/J_RoseBlack

bookbub.com/profile/j-rose-black

Also by J Rose Black

🩶 🎭 ROMANTIC COMEDY

Off the Record (Get it for free when you sign up for my newsletter): On the record, she's the world's most annoying reporter. Off the record, she's the one he can't let get away. ⚾🍿

SHORT STORY EBOOK

🌹 🔪 ROMANTIC SUSPENSE

Vengefully Yours (ebook, paperback, & audio) - a multiple award-winning collection of short romantic mystery-suspense stories. 🗡️🔍🖤

ROMANTIC SUSPENSE (CONT'D)

The Tell (Get it for free when you sign up for my newsletter!)

A short continuation from Dawn at La Seine (inside Vengefully Yours). 🔍 🕐 💰

SHORT STORY EBOOK

Join the ViP List

Scan the QR Code to sign up for my VIP list. It's a fun, no-spam community newsletter featuring <u>exclusive content</u>, giveaways and the latest news. Let's keep in touch!